A HIDDEN HEIR
TO REDEEM HIM

A HIDDEN HEIR
TO REDEEM HIM

DANI COLLINS

MILLS & BOON

First published in Great Britain 2020
by Mills & Boon, an imprint of HarperCollins*Publishers*
1 London Bridge Street, London, SE1 9GF

Large Print edition 2020

© 2020 Dani Collins

ISBN: 978-0-263-08493-1

MIX
Paper from
responsible sources
FSC™ C007454

This book is produced from independently certified FSC™ paper to ensure responsible forest management. For more information visit www.harpercollins.co.uk/green.

Printed and bound in Great Britain
by CPI Group (UK) Ltd, Croydon, CR0 4YY

In May of 2012 my editor
Megan Haslam phoned me
with an offer for my first sale to
Mills & Boon. Eight years later,
this is my thirty-fifth title. The longer
I do this, the more I appreciate the
entire team at Mills & Boon—
particularly Megan. Thank you
for this career, Megan. I absolutely
couldn't have done it without you.

CHAPTER ONE

VALENTINO CASALE HAD long ago hardened himself against useless things like feelings, but he found himself irritated by the congested streets of Athens.

Traffic was his driver's problem, not his, but he shifted restlessly, acknowledging the real pea beneath his mattress. Returning to Greece grated on him. Being sent here as a child had always felt like a punishment and still did. And to be thrust into the space between his father's money and his mother's grappling for it? That was the equivalent of being thrown into a cage with a hungry tiger.

So no, he was not pleased to be here.

This will be the last time, he assured himself with a grim look at the bustling mid-morning streets. At least his father wasn't here. *There* was a silver lining.

If he had feelings, Val supposed he would be experiencing grief or what some called "closure." Since receiving the news that Nikolai Mylonas had died two days ago, however, he had experienced no emotions at all, not even relief. His father would be cremated and his ashes interred on his island property. In lieu of a service that no one would attend, Nikolai's two sons and their mothers were requested to appear in person at the reading of his will.

Val had rejected any share in his father's wealth two decades ago. He'd built his own fortune off his own oiled back, *grazie*. He had even supplied his mother with a healthy allowance in hopes she would quit lusting after Niko's money, not that it had worked.

She had continued to take Niko's occasional checks and remained convinced that her son was entitled to *all* of his father's fortune. If she absolutely had to, she would settle for his receiving exactly 50 percent.

Val still didn't want it, as he had reiterated to his father's lawyer when the man had called to set up this meeting. Whatever he stood to inherit could be signed over to his mother if it couldn't be refused.

There were stipulations, he had been informed, that demanded the presence of all parties before anything could proceed.

The king was dead, but his legacy of manipulation lived on.

And yes, Val's mother was mentioned, the lawyer had hurried to state, so it was in Val's interest to show up and keep the wheels turning.

Who *cared* where the money went?

Evelina Casale, that was who. She cared about Niko's money above all things. She most especially cared how much she would receive as compared to Niko's ex-wife, Paloma. If the other woman was bequeathed so much as one euro more, well, Val supposed he would finally meet his half brother with pistols at dawn.

Another silver lining—

"Stop," he commanded, lifting his head off the back of his seat as his gaze caught the frontage of an art gallery. "Let me out here."

As he stepped from the car, his phone

dinged with another text from his mother, informing him she had arrived in the lobby.

She could wait. They all could.

He shoved his phone back into his pocket and crossed the street. Habit propelled him. For three years he had been entering every gallery he glimpsed, no matter what else was on his agenda. No matter if he'd been in the same shop days before.

Perversely, he was forever on the hunt for his own naked form and was always disappointed not to find it.

It didn't escape him that if he had wanted to embarrass his father with public nudes, he could have taken a photo down his drawers and posted it online years ago. Hell, in his heyday Val had modeled underwear so sheer and tight he might as well have been bare-assed, so any barb in such an act was long lost. At this point an unknown artist capitalizing on his notoriety by circulating a "classy" rendition of his junk was pure, pretentious vanity—which he was probably guilty of along with a multitude of other sins.

Alas, today was one more fruitless search.

He smirked at his own joke, but his humor was quickly overshadowed by aggravation. He ought to be pleased when he failed to find himself. Everyone used him to whatever extent they could. In this case he had blatantly given his permission to be exploited, but this one struggling artist hadn't done so.

Why not? It could have been the break she needed. As three years passed, however, and he failed to glimpse anything like her work again, a niggling concern had begun roiling in him that something had happened to her.

Why *that* might bother him, he couldn't fathom. His own father had died, and he had continued with the tennis game his mother's call with the news had interrupted.

There had been something about that young artist, though. She'd been both mature and self-reliant, yet naive. Charmingly open with her opinions and genuinely curious of his, unafraid to challenge his assumptions or have her own views picked apart. She hadn't taken anything from him, either. Not even the money he'd left for the sketch he'd ripped from her book and tucked into his briefcase so he wouldn't lose or crumple it.

His phone buzzed again. His mother was worried she might run into Paloma and Javiero before Val arrived.

As if Val would allow *them* to hurry him along. He didn't respond, only moved leisurely through the gallery, skimming his gaze across landscapes and abstracts, cats and fruit bowls and a view through a window that bore only the vaguest resemblance to the framed sketch hanging in his bedroom. The execution on this one wasn't nearly as skilled, and the signature was not the KO he sought.

One of these days he would go to Ireland and poke around their galleries, see if he was hanging out there.

He smirked again at his double entendre, but his glimmer of amusement fell away as he walked the final few blocks through blistering heat into the ninth circle of hell, otherwise known as the Mylonas office tower. He hadn't been here since, well, it must have been right before he'd flown to Venice three years ago, acting on a social media post that his father's rival was vacationing there.

Val wondered yet again whether he might have backed out of his ill-fated marriage if he'd come back to his hotel room after that initial meeting and found his unassuming artist still in his bed, rather than finding all the cash he'd had in his wallet still in its tidy stack on the night table, her and her sketch-book gone.

She'd been guileless and refreshingly oblivious to his position and money. He'd been utterly relaxed as she sketched him. It seemed ridiculous to say he had felt "safe." He was a powerful man with strength and position and money, rarely at a disadvantage, but it had been a surprising relief that he hadn't felt a need to keep his guard up with her.

He hadn't fully appreciated that until much later and to this day, he was annoyed with himself that he'd left her that morning, giving her a chance to disappear without a trace. He hadn't caught her last name and, with his father's ultimatum still ringing in his ears, he'd gone through with his plan to firmly divest of the old man once and for all.

That ruthless move had been the last time he'd allowed emotion to drive him. The "marry in haste" cliché had its roots in truth. He'd found no satisfaction in his marriage, only a sexless existence with a woman whose interests were not his own. At least their divorce was finalized, and he could turn the page on that chapter in his encyclopedic collection of sordid mistakes.

"Take your time," his mother said as he came through the revolving doors. She gave him a dismayed once-over. "Would a suit have killed you?"

"A suit would have implied this meeting was important to me."

She *tsked* and moved toward him from the waiting area, almost as tall as he was and still catwalk-thin at fifty-eight—though she would slay anyone who tried to claim she was a day over fifty-one. Of course, that would have made her pregnant at eighteen, when she'd been gracing the cover of swimsuit issues, but she reserved her math skills for counting calories and money.

"Good afternoon, Mr. Casale. I'm Nigel," one of his father's minions said. "May I escort you to the meeting room?" He waved them toward the bank of elevators.

Val turned and a megajolt of electricity shot through him as he was smacked in the eyes by the large oil behind the security desk.

"Where did that come from?" he demanded.

It hadn't been there three years ago. He had never seen it before in his life. The seascape framed by a window was unfamiliar, although the view itself had to be Greece. The blend of colors was new to his eyes, but they were gloriously understated while providing infinite texture and depth. Something in the composition was deeply familiar to him, too. The waft of the curtain in the breeze was reminiscent of the drape of a charcoal shirt over the back of a chair.

The painting was so bizarrely evocative of *her*, she might as well have stood next to him, whispering in his ear, telling him that she felt safe in here, but the wildness beyond called to her. This painting was a threshold of sorts, as she contemplated moving into a new world filled with uncertainty, but also with vast and glorious new experiences.

"You can't come back here, sir."

He brushed past the security guard and examined the signature. Not the KO on his own sketch, but *Kiara*. His skin tightened all over his body.

"Where did you get this? I want to speak to this artist." He didn't ask himself why, but when the security guard only gave a baffled shrug, Val wanted to punch him.

"Um, sir?" Nigel the minion offered a perplexed look. "Miss O'Neill is upstairs. She arrived for your meeting ten minutes ago."

"For the reading of my father's will?" His scalp prickled. The sensation kept going, lifting a sharp tingle along the sides of his neck and running the length of his spine. His gut knotted and his groin twitched. His skin felt too tight for the heat that was suddenly pressurizing inside him, crystalizing the carbon in his body tissue to diamond hardness.

"Who is she?" his mother asked at a distance.

Val barely heard her over his harsh laugh of outraged, gallows humor.

"Someone who worked for Dad." How had he missed that? Blinded by his own libido, he supposed. Cursing himself, he said, "Yes. By all means. Take me to her. I. Can't. Wait."

Kiara O'Neill could tell that Niko's lawyer, Davin, was trying to put her at ease with his incessant small talk, but it wasn't working. Maybe he thought he was charming her? They'd met several times in the past three years and he had invited her to dinner more than once, but her priorities were always her daughter and her art, in that order. If she squeezed in an evening of wine and a rom-com with her best friend, Scarlett, she considered her life complete.

Trying to fit a man into her narrow world would only complicate her to-do list. Besides, the last time she'd gone on a date, she'd wound up pregnant.

And the man in question would enter this boardroom any second.

Her whole body was soaked in a clammy sweat, her mind incapable of holding a sensible thought, let alone a conversation. Her belted dress and flowing kimono jacket, chosen so carefully to be unobtrusive and comfortable while offering an impression of quiet confidence, felt constrictive. Her unsettled stomach was full of snakes, and the feminist inside her who had happily told men to talk to her hand for three years was wringing said hands like an adolescent girl when the grad ball was announced. The cute boy was coming down the corridor and she didn't know if she wanted him to notice her or not.

She kept thinking she should have done something different with her hair. Straightened it, maybe. She should have worn more makeup, to disguise her apprehension. Or maybe not so much, so she didn't look so... polished. Niko had liked her to look and sound and act a certain way and she'd gone along with it because, ugh, *reasons*, but this wasn't who she was.

Deep down she was still a mixed race orphan from Cork's dodgiest neighborhood. Scarlett would point out she was actually a mother and an artist, but Kiara was faking her way through both of those things so she wasn't sure they counted.

Val Casale had seemed like a smart man. She suspected he would see straight through to the fraud she was, no matter how she presented herself.

Although, he had seemed to think her work had genuine merit. When she had demurred, he'd said, "You really don't know who I am, do you?"

She hadn't. Not until much later.

It was all coming home to roost now, though.

She concentrated on not licking the lipstick off her mouth. Her throat was dry, making it impossible to swallow. All morning her heart rate had been picking up to a panicked speed, then petering out in a cold flush, leaving her light-headed and vaguely exhausted. She worried she would faint any second and reminded herself yet again to *breathe*. She didn't want to be stroked out on the floor when Val walked in.

She wanted to text Scarlett to hurry back from the ladies' room, but she had already set her phone to silent and tucked it into her clutch. Pulling it out midconversation would be rude.

With a stiff smile she fought to keep in place, she waited for Davin to pause in his rattling on, planning to say something about checking on Scarlett. Scarlett was heavily pregnant. It wasn't strange that she pretty much lived in the ladies' room these days, but she was taking a long time. Had she bumped into some of their guests? Was today's meeting taking place out there without her?

Had Val already heard the news and walked away, before he'd laid eyes on her or offered her a chance to explain? Given everything she'd heard about him since, that was probably for the best, but her heart twisted in anguish on behalf of—

The door opened and the air changed in a subtle rush. A thrust of tense energy came in with the three people who entered.

"*Signor* and *Signora* Casale," Nigel announced, glancing at his tablet as it dinged. "The other party has arrived. I'll return with them shortly." He melted away, closing the door.

"Davin." Val's mother, Evelina, sounded as frosty and cultured as she had the one time Kiara had spoken to her three years ago. In person, Evelina was the epitome of what fashion magazines deemed sexy and attractive, nearly six foot and wispy. She had ivory skin and lustrous brunette hair that shimmered as she floated down the far side of the table. Her clothes were designer, her neck and ears and fingers bedecked in glittering jewels. She greeted Davin with perfunctory air kisses.

"Evelina. Lovely to see you again," Davin said politely before introducing Kiara. "This is Kiara O'Neill."

Evelina's gaze skimmed past her with a dismissive, "Water will do for now."

Kiara might have been amused—or insulted—but a millennium's worth of fireworks were going off inside her at the sight of Valentino Casale. Every emotion possible whistled and burst in her ears while sparks and flashes of color exploded in her vision.

He hadn't bothered with a suit. He wore ripped jeans and a black shirt open at the throat. They clung to a frame that was every bit as athletically lean and flawless as it had been three years ago. His hair was still tousled, his jaw still in need of a shave.

His gaze was exactly as piercing and unsettling. His silvery irises—endearingly familiar—pinned onto her, unwavering and fierce.

Adrenaline urged her to run for her life, but the sting was laced with a bizarre excitement. An urge to run *to* him. Between those imperatives sat a mixture of more complex emotions. Cavernous guilt and angry resentment and something like painful relief.

She had dreaded and anticipated this day from the moment she had agreed to Niko's offer to live with him. She would finally confront Val about their daughter. She had braced for whatever consequences that might produce, but she hadn't braced for the effect Val still had on her.

Profound attraction accosted her. She

shouldn't be surprised. The first time she'd seen him, he'd caused a stab of irresistible fascination in her. Time had stopped and her blood had sizzled as she had begun caressing the lines of his face in velvety shades of charcoal.

That same sensual yank took hold of her today, but stronger. It was deeper, immediate and sexual. Not simply a compulsion to study and re-create him on a page, but a gut-deep desire to close the distance and touch him. She wanted to feel him with her entire body and bask in the fire he lit inside her. She wanted to feel the sweep of his hands down her naked back and his strong grip on her hips.

Her body heated and tingled and grew aroused simply by standing in a room with him because she knew what making love with him felt like. She knew how he could make her feel—animalistic and alluring and *good*.

She hadn't calculated the effect of their connection through their child, either. She had spent over two years living with his father and his daughter. She knew so much more about Val Casale now, yet she still didn't know *him*. Her brief crush and the memory of a sweet encounter had become a spellbinding enthrallment with someone who had had a profound effect on her life.

Despite the things she'd been told about him, however, and despite the fact he'd ultimately slighted and discarded her, everything within her wanted to reach out and rediscover the sexy, hedonistic man she'd glimpsed that night.

The indulgent smile of her lover was gone, though. His cynicism and contempt were palpable in the polished chrome of his gaze.

Did he know that she'd had their baby? Was that why he was throwing accusation at her like bolts of lightning with his bitter look?

His antagonism was obvious. Her stomach bottomed out as she recalled one of the first things Niko had told her about his son.

Val is a bastard, Miss O'Neill. He takes pride in the distinction and seizes every opportunity to live down to the label.

At different times Niko had used all manner of unsavory descriptors—disrespectful, rebellious, confrontational, reprehensible, *vengeful.*

He hadn't been a man one contradicted, even though his view of Val hadn't sounded like the man she'd met. Regardless, anger with his father had prompted Val to turn his back on a fortune and marry a woman he didn't love. That made him a man no sensible woman would cross.

And Niko might have offered her protection from Val while he'd been alive, but Niko was gone. Kiara was on her own.

Davin broke the thick silence by setting down the jug of water with a clunk. He held out the glass to Evelina, who ignored it as she stared between them.

"Do you know each other?" Evelina asked.

Kiara's arteries stung with a fresh release of fight or flight. She looked to the door, willing Scarlett to appear.

"What are you doing here, Kiara?" Val's voice, for all its lethal sharpness, was still deep enough to invoke a sense of curling into a soft bed under a thick quilt.

She glanced at Davin.

"When all mentioned parties are present, we'll discuss the particulars of dispersal," Davin said with a twitch of a smile that died on contact under Evelina's death-ray glare.

"Do not tell me this...*person*...is entitled to some portion of Niko's estate?" Evelina's outraged gaze went down Kiara's ample curves in pale yellow and summer-sky blue. Her lip curled with distaste.

"Not exactly," Kiara croaked, snatching up her own glass of ice water and dampening her throat. "I should check on Scarlett." Perhaps they could hide together in the ladies' room until this blew over.

Before she could take a step toward the door, however, it flung open.

"Very sorry," Nigel stammered. "There's been a development. Miss Walker has gone to the hospital."

"What? Why? What happened?" In her shock, Kiara misjudged the height of the table. Her glass tipped as she set it down on her way to the door. The puddle of water streaked out alongside her as the glass rolled toward Val on the other side of the table. He caught it before it fell and shattered.

"She's in labor," Nigel said. "*Señor* Rodriguez has taken her. His mother has chosen not to stay. The, uh, central message of this meeting was, um, conveyed by Miss Walker and…" Nigel glanced uncomfortably toward Evelina then swung his attention back to Kiara. "She said to tell you to finish your business here and call her when you're able."

Of course she had. Scarlett never thought of herself.

"I'll leave you to it," Nigel said, drawing the door closed on his exit.

"Do *not*—" Evelina flung around with ominous warning toward Davin "—tell me that some gold digger is having Paloma's grandchild and all of Niko's money is going to *them*." Tears of rage glittered in her eyes.

Val, on the other hand, gave an ironic snort. A dent of acrid humor twitched one corner of his mouth. "Touché, Javiero," he drawled.

"Not…um…all of it." Davin hurried to mollify Evelina. He flashed a cautious glance at Kiara. "Perhaps we should sit?"

"I'll stand." Kiara grasped the back of a chair to steady herself while the world spun off its axis around her. Her mind was splintering with concern for her best friend while her heart hammered as the moment of truth arrived like a cliff before her. Her toes curled to keep her from tumbling over it, but she was going to fall regardless.

Her eyes clung to the punishing contact in Valentino's unrelenting stare. She watched comprehension dawn the way clouds parted and the sun suddenly pierced through in a shaft of brilliant, searing hot light.

A whooshing sensation tipped her past the point of no return. She couldn't speak, but she didn't have to.

"Calm down, Mother." His tone descended to a grim, deadly rasp. "This gold digger has also had a child."

"Sir," the lawyer admonished, but Val didn't let the man's disapproval impact him. He was suffering too—a sharp sting of betrayal.

Kiara had presented herself as a sensual,

self-deprecating, penniless artist with a heart that he now realized had been iron pyrite.

And he was the fool who'd believed in her.

He'd thought they'd enjoyed a chance encounter, one where he hadn't needed to deflect or overpower the situation in order to keep control of it. He had thought they had shared, if not secrets, a lack of lies.

She had haunted him.

And she'd been working for his father the whole time.

She had been more than Eve with an apple; she'd been the snake, slithering her way into his periphery, seemingly harmless then turning on him when he least suspected it. How was he surprised? *How?* And *of course* his father had played the long con. Of course he had.

But how had they managed it? Had she already been working for his father when they met? Had Niko hired her to lure Val into bed and get her pregnant?

Nice work if you can get it. And lucky shot to make it happen in one go and only because one of the condoms broke.

"You have a child?" His mother clawed a pale hand at the diamonds around her throat.

"Yes." Kiara's knuckles stood out like brass bullets where her brown hands clutched the back of a chair.

Her hair was longer, parted on one side. Light played through the brown-gold mass of springs that were so fine and narrow, each strand looked as though it had been wound around a pencil or something smaller. The coils piled upon themselves in wild abandon around her oval face, accentuating her high cheekbones.

Her big eyes were pools of espresso, her mouth a round pout painted in brick red. Had she had elocution lessons? Or had the broad Irish accent she'd used that night been a put-on to trick him into believing she was the harmless backpacker she'd pretended to be?

Her teeth had been straightened, but the rest of her was still mouthwateringly curvaceous, draped in clothes of a much higher quality than the last time he'd seen her. She wore heels so she seemed taller than he remembered. A wide belt at her waist emphasized the thrust of her breasts and the generous flare of her round hips and bottom.

A very carnal memory threatened to take hold and dull his wits all over again. Sex was only sex, he reminded himself. It was a pleasant pastime to be enjoyed like dessert or sailing on a hot day, not something that should be used against others the way she had clearly used it against him—on his father's behalf—*damn her to hell*.

"Since things have taken such a sharp turn, I'll come straight to the point," Davin said, fingering through the papers before him. "Given that both of Nikolai's sons have renounced their claim to his fortune, he has bequeathed the bulk of his estate in equal parts to his grandchildren. Obviously, we're wishing everything goes well with Miss Walker's delivery. With that happy event, to the best of our knowledge, there will be two heirs who will share equally in the assets. Evelina and Paloma have been allotted a one-time, one-million-euro payment." Davin slid a cashier's check toward Val's mother. "Each."

"One— That's not enough!" she cried.

"Sounds like you'll have to be nicer to Kiara," Val said, drinking deeply of that satire. "Don't assume she's only here to fetch your beverages, for instance."

"This can't be right." His mother hurried to Davin's side and demanded to read it with her own eyes.

Val met Kiara at the end of the table.

"You understand what this means?" he asked, jerking his head to indicate his mother. "She will never let you rest. I thought you were on the pill," he recalled.

Kiara's shoulders twitched, but any guilt was short-lived. Her gaze sparked with affront as she met his.

"We're doing that here? Now?" Her cheeks darkened with a blush. "It was a low dose to regulate my cycle. When I spent the night with you, I missed one. Apparently, it was enough to disrupt the effectiveness. There's no such thing as a perfect contraceptive, you know."

"My father didn't pay you to spend the night with me and get pregnant?"

"And break the condom? No." She rocked back a step, scowling as if insulted.

"If you knew him well enough to pry half his assets out of him, you know he would be capable of something like that." Look at the disregard Niko was showing toward the mothers of both his sons right now, throwing them a token settlement while he enriched the women who gave him grandchildren. Niko had been unswayed by sentiment. Ruthless. "Did you sleep with him?"

"*No*. That's a disgusting suggestion."

"Says the woman using a baby to get her hands on a fortune."

Her chin came up in a tiny signal of challenge.

Challenge accepted, *tesoro*.

Why? He didn't care.

He shouldn't care, at any rate.

But he discovered that he did. Deeply. Emotions he couldn't name were churning in his gut.

"You pretended you didn't know who I was that night," he accused.

She had seemed charmingly unaware when

he had told her his name, but at the time he'd been weighing the idea of marriage to a stranger. Obviously, she'd taken advantage of his distraction.

"You skipped the pill on purpose, in hopes of winning the jackpot? Such tactics have been tried in the past, with limited success." He sent a mocking wave down his front. "You'll come to regret this."

"Having my daughter?" she asked with another lofty notch of her chin. "I doubt it. She has a name, by the way. Would you like to hear it?"

"No." He could have exited on that. The man he had cultivated himself into nearly always stole the last word and tossed a match over his shoulder as he walked away.

Something kept him rooted, however, listening for the name. Waiting for Kiara to take another shot at him. He didn't know why, but he wanted both. He wanted to stay right here, feeling the streaking pinball of incendiary energy continue to heat as it bounced between them.

How could she still hold such a spell over

him when he now knew her to be mercenary and devious.

"I told him to give you the money you needed to take care of it," Evelina spat from the other side of the room. "He said you *did*."

Val had been in enough scraps to duck any punch, but that one suckered him. His abs belatedly clenched as he snapped a look at his mother. "You *knew* about this?"

"You didn't?" Kiara's gaze flashed back to his with wary confusion.

"I knew she was claiming to be pregnant with your child. I didn't know she *had* it." Evelina glared censure at Kiara.

Kiara's lashes swept down again, and her mouth firmed as she pronounced with dignity, "Niko *has* given me money to take care of her."

Evelina caught her breath as she realized how badly she had misplayed her hand.

Val should have found that hilarious, but learning of his mother's involvement had taken him by the throat and shaken him.

"You knew she was pregnant? And you didn't tell me?" he demanded of her.

"You were on your honeymoon." His mother's voice dropped to the syrupy, conciliatory tone that wheedled for him to take her side. "You didn't need an ugly scandal."

"Like the one I grew up in?" When had he last bothered to be angry? Truly furious? Maybe his last visit to this tower? Maybe it was the air in here that stoked his rage. The fetid stench of manipulation and jealousy and profound selfishness. "You live for making a scene. Blaming Niko for my shortcomings is your bread and butter. You could have used the baby for leverage all this time if you had— Oh, my God."

Val hooked his hands on his hips and laughed drily toward the ceiling as he realized why she had preferred his baby be erased from existence.

"This is a new low for you, Mother." He was uncharacteristically, profoundly astounded. And sickened. "Or should I say… Nonna?"

"Do *not*…" she warned in shaken outrage.

"Oh, I will. Because your precious vanity sent *her* to *him*." He pointed at Kiara then the folder representing the fortune that had been the reason for, and the bane of, his very existence.

This situation was abhorrently reminiscent of his childhood, when something clean and precious and *his* would be sullied and used as leverage and snapped apart in the struggle between his parents and his half brother and his father's ex-wife, Paloma. Val's wants and needs had never been part of any conversation. If they had, they'd been dismissed as irrelevant.

And Kiara had played along with all of that.

"Why did you tell her instead of me?" he demanded of Kiara.

Whatever culpability flickered into Kiara's face was quickly schooled into something more facetious. "I guess I could have left a message with your *wife*?"

It was a darling effort at shaming him, but, "I've been divorced a year. You've had time."

"There were circumstances." She shifted uncomfortably. "Niko was ill and needed us there."

"You've been *living* with him? This whole time?"

If Val believed people were capable of true remorse, he might have thought the way Kiara bit her lip might have signaled regret.

He had played this game too long to believe she felt anything but glee, however, at claiming the pot of gold.

Walk away, he thought. *Just. Walk. Away.*

"He thought if you knew Aurelia existed, you would pressure me to leave the island instead of staying with him."

Aurelia. It was the name of the villa in Venice where they'd spent their night together. The site of their lovemaking and, apparently, the conception of their daughter.

Every morning, when he gazed on Kiara's sketch, he was back there on the bed with her, seated behind her in the rumpled sheets, teasing her into continuing with her study of the open balcony doors while he sampled the scent in her neck and tasted the smoothness of her shoulders and felt her breast rise and fall in growing excitement against his palm.

He swallowed, trying to dismiss any profundity in her bestowing that villa's name on their child. He didn't buckle to sentiment. It was a manipulation tactic. Everything was.

Even so, he couldn't take his eyes off her as she turned her attention to his mother, showing no fear as she said baldly, "Niko didn't want you or Paloma to know about her or about Scarlett's pregnancy. He thought it would create more conflict than he could deal with in his weakened condition. Since he was terminal, we respected his wishes."

It was so poetic, it bordered on sappy, but to keep the knowledge of his daughter from him for *three years*? He would never forgive any of them for this.

"We'll wait for a DNA test before we continue this discussion." Evelina took care to tuck her cashier's check into her clutch. "Niko can't overlook his son in favor of a child we've never seen. We'll fight this."

"You'll be wasting your money," Davin said. "There's already a DNA test that proves Aurelia is Niko's descendant. Her sample was correlated with the DNA test that proved Mr. Casale's paternity. Niko was of sound mind. Further tests won't change anything."

Val didn't need a test. He wasn't so gullible as to take Kiara's word, but his father had always been diligent about such fine points.

He didn't care anyway, he assured himself. Not beyond how galling it was that Niko had gotten the last laugh, but so what? Val had never wanted offspring—one of the reasons his marriage had tanked—and he hadn't wanted his father's money, either. He had no desire to take responsibility for the child in possession of that fortune— Oh, wait. The girl was only entrusted with half. That meant any involvement he had with her would mean dealing with Javiero on some level, as well.

And all the while, his mother would continue to claw at him for her piece of the pie.

Definitely time to exit stage right. He certainly could. Kiara was financially equipped to meet the needs of his child. Nothing in his life had to change. In fact, his mother would become Kiara's problem. The solution was elegantly simple and utterly freeing.

Yet, he remained where he was, coldly enraged. His insides were gripped by a wrath that swelled his chest with the pressure of a primal yell he couldn't release.

He could hardly pick apart why this provoked such a volcanic rise of fury in him. It had something to do with the grotesque replay of history. While he'd been married to Tina, Kiara had been having his child, sentencing an innocent to the label he'd worn like a dead albatross until he was old enough to make damn sure he deserved the slur.

No. He might not have crafted himself into the most upstanding of men, but he was decent enough to pluck a child out of a toxic spill before she was lethally poisoned and scarred forever.

"Refuse that money," he told Kiara. "My daughter will inherit *my* fortune, not his."

"A minute ago you didn't even want to know her name."

"She can have *mine*," he shot back. "You're going to marry me. *Today.*"

CHAPTER TWO

"VAL. DON'T BE RASH." The whites of Evelina's eyes showed. "We'll fight this—"

"Take your money and go home, Mother. I'll call when I'm ready to speak to you again."

Evelina wasn't rattled, but Val's tone had Kiara shaking in her designer heels. She was doing her best to channel Scarlett, who never ruffled, but Kiara regularly lost battles against her two-year-old. She had folded like a cheap tent when Niko had dragged her into this arrangement, hadn't she? She was no match for Val.

And marriage? Of all the reactions she had tried to anticipate... No, she wouldn't let herself process that. She was still absorbing the fact he hadn't known she had been pregnant. That seriously undermined her ability to resent him and take the high ground.

"Kiara can't refuse the money," Davin said. "It's Aurelia's. When she takes full control at twenty-five, Aurelia can do what she likes. Until then, the money remains in trust for her. A reasonable allowance is allocated to Miss O'Neill so she can provide Aurelia a stable home and upbringing. There's also a provision for a financial manger's salary. Miss Walker was intending to act in that capacity—"

"The Miss Walker currently birthing my half brother's heir? Hell, no," Val stated.

"Scarlett *is* in labor." Kiara's brain had been splintering with worry for her best friend this whole time. "And I'm her birth coach. I need to go to the hospital."

She would take her friend's place in the stirrups if it would grant her an escape from the malevolence coming off Val in waves.

"Hell, no again," he said, tone implacable. "The last time you disappeared, you had my child and conspired with my parents to hide her from me for *three years*."

Kiara had one decent coping strategy for confrontation—sarcasm.

"Did we have sex today? I didn't notice." She blinked. "You do move fast, I recall, but I think we're safe this time."

Val set his hands on the table, pushing a force field over and around her, trapping her with his dangerous mood inside an airless bubble.

"Shall I recite everything *I* remember from our night together?"

A fluttering swirl of erotic memory accosted the pit of her belly. Heat flowed into secretive spaces and her nipples pinched. Why had she thought silk was a good choice? He could probably see the effect his words had on her. He was a practiced seducer, after all.

One who was, perhaps, entitled to his outrage. She had been hurt by his cavalier treatment, but keeping Aurelia's birth a secret from him had never felt right. From the moment she had known she was pregnant she had wanted to tell him about their daughter. So far, his reaction wasn't very encouraging. It wasn't very *personal*, but she had always

cherished a small dream that he would ultimately fall in love with their daughter.

Why? Because of her own fatherless upbringing? Ugh. Daddy issues were so clichéd.

"Replays won't be necessary," she mumbled
as she gathered her clutch and looked for the
bag she usually carried, the one bulked with
art supplies and baby wipes, snacks and clean
clothes. She was traveling light today, having
planned for a brief meeting and a quick bolt
back to the island.

"I have to make some calls," she said, realizing she would have her first night away
from her daughter while Scarlett brought her
own infant into the world. "I'll leave you to
wrap up?"

Davin nodded and Evelina turned with umbrage toward him, but Val met Kiara at the
door.

"Thank you," she murmured as he held it
for her.

He followed her through it and sparks con-
densed in the air between them as he paced
her down the hall to the elevator.

"Um…" She started to ask him what he was doing, but it was obvious he was leaving.

He took out his phone to make a call as they waited for the elevator.

She took out her own phone and saw Scarlett's texts. She read them as they stepped into the elevator.

My water broke. Help!

That one must have been sent from the ladies' room. Kiara could have kicked herself for silencing her phone when she had entered the boardroom.

Javiero's mother just came in. What do I do?

Then:

Javiero is taking me to hosp. Call me when you can.

Kiara bit back a groan of contrition and dialed.

Beside her, Val told someone, "I want to get married. No, not here. Italy."

As her jaw dropped, and the elevator hit the

bottom floor, rocking her on her heels, Scarlett answered in her ear.

"Are you okay?" Kiara asked her dumbly, watching Val tuck his phone into his pocket.

His gaze held hers as he leaned on the door to brace it open, trapping her where she stood.

"I'm in labor, what do you think?" Scarlett groaned. "Oh, my *Gawd*, how did you do this?"

"I'm on my way," Kiara promised, forced to brush against Val's intimidating frame as she stepped from the elevator. Another shower of tingles washed over her. "Leaving the office now."

"Wait." Scarlett made a helpless noise. "Javiero wants to stay with me."

"Okay." Kiara halted in the middle of the lobby. "What do *you* want?"

"I don't *know*! I had to tell him everything and now he thinks you shouldn't be here." A small hesitation, then, "Because of Val."

Val paused to loom beside her, probably able to hear every word.

Until today, she had understood there was animosity between the men, but after Evelina's resentful reaction, and the grate in his words as he'd pronounced "my half brother's spawn," she had a clearer picture of how much genuine dislike existed between them.

"Listen." Kiara gentled her tone as she spoke to Scarlett, reminding herself that her friend's delivery wasn't about her. "If you want Javiero there, that's fine. I completely understand. If my coming to the hospital will cause you more stress than comfort, I'll go to a hotel and stand by. If you decide you want me, call. It doesn't matter if it's the middle of the night. I'll come. Sound good?"

"Thank you," Scarlett said on a little sob. "I'm a wreck and— Oh, here comes another one." She sucked in a breath. A male voice said something, and she replied with a petulant, "I *am* breathing. What do you know about it? Oh, my God, I *hate* you for doing this to me."

The call ended, presumably cut off by Javiero taking the phone from Scarlett.

Kiara frowned with concern as she tucked away her phone.

"It takes two weeks," Val said.

"Labor? Mine was fourteen hours."

"Marriage." He narrowed his eyes at her remark, but continued, "We can do it faster elsewhere, like here in Greece, but I want to marry in Italy."

"Or not at all," she suggested with a falsely bright smile, even though a weight of anger that had been sitting on her lungs for three years had shifted and angled deeper into her heart, leaving a painful ache.

She avoided the flash in his eyes by striding across to the security desk.

"I need my car and a reservation at a hotel near the hospital."

"My driver is here." Val nodded at the black sedan that halted against the curb beyond the glass front of the building.

Kiara opened her mouth to protest, but he said darkly, "We're not finished, Kiara. We haven't even started."

She swallowed a groan of resignation and went with him.

Beside him, Kiara was telling someone that Scarlett had gone into labor. "A little early, yes, but only a week or so. I'll stay the night here in case she needs me. Is Aurelia napping? Call me when she's up. I'll text you when I have news. Thank you."

"Where is she?" Val asked, barely processing that he had a child, still blinded by the conspiracy of lies and secrecy that had kept her hidden from him.

"The island. That was one of her nannies."

"One of," he repeated. "Does she even know who 'Mama' is?" He skimmed his glance over tailored silk and pearl buttons, a vintage handbag and a contemporary Italian designer's shoe that featured a gold wristwatch as an ankle band. "I know couture when I see it. And I know guilt when I see it, too," he remarked as her expression tightened.

"A mother is automatically issued a stone's worth of guilt for every ounce of child." Her chin notched up as she looked forward. "Especially if she works. You get double if working isn't necessary for survival. And if the job you do is creative and doesn't pay by the hour? I need a freight train to carry it all."

Val's mother had never been burdened with

such inconvenient emotions as guilt, but Evelina was in a constant battle against excess weight of any kind.

Kiara didn't diet herself skeletal. Her body was luscious and ripe.

He had thought his reaction to her three years ago had been more about burning off the tension of the decision he'd made to marry a stranger, but sitting next to her, detecting her scent beneath the light fragrance of her cosmetics, was affecting him. He had to shift to make room behind his fly, which aggravated him. He didn't lust after any woman. He enjoyed sex, but desire was one more feeling that could be used to manipulate. He preferred free will and he sure as hell wasn't letting this woman have any advantages over him again.

Even so, his gaze snagged on her knee and he recalled vividly the softness of her skin, the way it warmed under his caress and tasted rose petal-soft against his lips. The pull in his groin sharpened.

Kiara flicked at the hem of her dress to

cover her knee. Her gaze swept up to see if he had noticed and clashed into his.

Yes, he was aware of the woman beneath the clothes, he conveyed. Sex was never a power game for him, but she had started this one. And if anyone knew how to weaponize sex and win that game, it was a man who'd sold everything from fragrance to tuxedos with a bared chest and a libidinous pout.

He let his eyelids drop to a sultry half-mast and touched his tongue to his bottom lip. The muscles in his face were as well exercised and disciplined as those in his chest and abs and thighs. He softened his expression into admiration. Approval. Come hither, my beauty.

"Feel guilty for letting my father dress you," he said of the muted yellow dress that had Niko's stamp of conservative authority all over it. "I'll find you more flattering colors and styles." He indulged himself with a thorough study of her unabashed curves.

Her breasts rose in a shaken catch of breath, and the way her nipples stood up against the silk caused a responding stiffening in his pants.

She didn't notice his reaction. Her eyes had gone so wide as she looked into his face, he could practically count each of her thickened lashes. Color darkened her cheekbones. She looked away and swallowed loud enough that he heard it.

That swift, exquisitely sensual response was exactly what had ensnared him the first time. The way she had caught her lip in a soft bite after the graze of their fingertips as they discussed her sketches. The longing in her eyes as she had traversed his nude form with her gaze, transferring what she saw to the page.

Had that reaction been real or was it something in her playbook? She was averting her eyes so he couldn't be sure.

"Niko insisted I needed a proper wardrobe," she stammered with an ingenue's waver of uncertainty cracking her voice. "Since I've been going back and forth to Paris, we shopped there. We always take Aurelia, though."

"We?" His naturally possessive nature rose to a new level with that tiny word.

"Scarlett and I," she clarified with a wary flick of her glance.

"She's really having that SOB's kid? She does go above and beyond, doesn't she?"

"Scarlett is having Javiero's baby, yes." Her spine straightened, thrusting her breasts out. "She's also my friend so I would appreciate if you spoke more kindly about her."

He snorted. "How did it come about? Aside from the obvious. Did Dad pay *her* to get knocked up?"

"*No.* Where do you get the idea women run around getting pregnant for money?"

"Not all women perhaps, but in this family, it's all too common. I am the embodiment of such a tactic, and Paloma married my father and had Javiero because her family was broke."

"Well I took precautions that failed and Scarlett can speak for herself on that topic if she so chooses. I won't gossip about her, but try to have some empathy. These last weeks have been very difficult. Her pregnancy wasn't the easiest, Niko was in his final days, and you know that Javiero just got out of the hospital?"

"I saw the headlines."

Val wasn't pleased that his half brother had nearly been killed by a jaguar. Javiero had lost an eye if reports were accurate. Sounded damned hellish, but caring in any way about what happened on that side of his father's gene pool was a recipe for madness so Val hadn't let himself dwell on it.

They arrived at his hotel and, moments later, he watched her get her bearings much as she had three years ago, when he had brought her into his suite in Venice. She moved through the grand space with every indication she was absorbing minute details. She touched the tassel on the corner of a cushion, lifted her gaze to ornate plaster at the top of the walls, tipped her head into a floral arrangement and moved the curtain, watching where the light fell.

She removed her kimono jacket and went to stand at the window, tilting her head as she studied the Acropolis. He hung back and let his gaze wander her soft shoulders and the tuck of her waist and that glorious bottom pressing against silk that was weightless as a cobweb against her curves.

His palms twitched and so did hers.

She glanced around, gave a muted sigh.

"Is that why you did it?" he asked, instinctively knowing she was looking for her sketch pad. Her compulsion to capture an image was as strong as her ability to do so. He'd learned that much about her in their short acquaintance. "My father supported your art? I saw the painting in the lobby."

Her lips parted and culpability flexed across her expression.

"*I* gave you a stepladder," he reminded through gritted teeth.

"And I may have resorted to selling those sketches if your father hadn't offered to support me, but he did." She rolled her bottom lip inward and chewed it without mercy.

"When? Were you working for him when we met?"

"*No,*" she insisted, but he would reserve judgment on how much truth her words held. "And I didn't mean to get pregnant. I honestly thought I was protected. By the time I found out, you were on your honeymoon."

"So you called my mother and told her you planned to terminate."

"Are you judging me for that?"

"I'm judging you for telling everyone *but* me that you were pregnant with my child."

"Your mother was the only person I told," she muttered, looking at her short, unpainted fingernails. "And I only called her because I felt quite desperate, financially and emotionally." She frowned. "I didn't have any family or even a network of friends. I had no idea what sort of mother I might turn into since it had never been my plan to become one. I had put Venice on my credit card and had other debts. I'm not proud of that, but I'm not ashamed, either. Until I turned up pregnant, art was all that mattered to me. I took whatever job bought me a meat pie and colored pencils, not necessarily in that order. I didn't have a flat, just a room with a shared kitchen and bath. That standard of living was fine for me, but I knew I couldn't bring a child into it. I didn't have the education to get a better job, though. I can barely type and even graphic designers need computer skills. Putting 'currently pregnant' on your CV doesn't get you a lot of job offers. I would have had to rely on benefits from the state for years to get on my feet. I'd already spent most of my childhood on government assistance. I had to explore all my options, no matter how hard that sounds, so I called your mother. I thought that, since she'd been in a similar situation, she might have some empathy, perhaps offer other solutions."

"Well, aren't you charmingly naive?" Val's mother had been Nikolai Mylonas's long-suffering mistress right up until the day Niko had married Paloma. Val didn't know if she had poked holes in condoms or if his father had misjudged her desire to preserve her figure, but Evelina had turned up pregnant about the time Nikolai's bride had conceived. Val had been a deliberate effort on Evelina's part to stake a claim on Niko's fortune, but Niko had had two sons by two different women two days apart.

The war over rights of succession had raged ever since.

"Your mother said that my having your baby would ruin your life as well as my own and that I should never contact her again," Kiara said somberly. "But she must have called Niko because Scarlett called me a few hours later and turned up the next day. She talked me into coming to Greece to meet him."

Ah, Scarlett. His father's infinitely polite and pathologically single-minded enforcer.

"Niko was in treatment and said both his sons had turned his back on him. He wanted an heir and said your child would do nicely. He offered to build me a studio. It was an offer I didn't want to resist, but the most compelling reason I stayed was simply that he was Aurelia's family. I wanted to give her that. I won't say he was doting or openly loving, but he was proud of her in his way. It seemed like the right thing to do."

"You thought it was morally correct to let him into her life even though he kept you from telling *me*. Her *father*."

"For all I knew, you knew and didn't care!"

she said with a spark of temper. "The way you've reacted so far has only reinforced that Niko was right. You would have pressured me to take sides."

"You did take a side. His."

"I see it as taking turns." Her strident tone came down a few notches. "Niko's time was finite. Having Aurelia in his life brought him a sense of peace in his last days."

"How nice for him."

"You knew he was sick! You could have come at any time and would have learned you had a daughter."

"Is that his oversimplified rationalization or yours? Dad knew I wouldn't come and so did Scarlett. That logic doesn't wash."

"Why did you hate him so much?" she asked with bafflement.

He might have withstood the comparisons to his brother, the harsh punishments and the constant demands for good, better, best. What Val could never forgive was Niko overriding the complaint Val had made against the school's administration. Niko had had the entire thing dismissed as 'troublemaking' on Val's part so it was swept under the rug.

Val had never felt so helpless and furious in his life. So abandoned. Out of sheer desperation, he'd begun a campaign of unrelenting fighting and pranks and drinking until the school had had to throw him out for good.

"Why the hell did you *like* him? Why did you think he deserved time with my daughter more than I did?" It incensed him to imagine his father basking in the satisfaction of stealing those moments and milestones from Val.

"He was *dying.*" Her voice softened to a plea. "He was diagnosed right before… Venice. I know he didn't tell you that at the time. When I met him, though, he was quite sick. Weak and scared. I didn't plan to stay in Greece, but I couldn't leave."

"I'm sure it was a difficult choice."

"It wasn't *greed,*" she cried.

"Oh, I don't blame you for taking whatever incentives he offered," he assured her. "If he hadn't gotten you with the honey of money, he would have moved on to more aggressive and oppressive methods." He moved behind the bar to select a bottle of whiskey. "That's the sort of man I remember and I know he was. Controlling. Demanding."

If you leave, you're taking your mother with you. I won't support her. That will be up to you so button your lip and appreciate the education you're being given.

"I rejected his fortune, so I didn't have to bow to him the way you have. You think I don't see him in all of this?" He drew a circle around the conservative ensemble and the way she was justifying actions that were unjustifiable. "He kept you on the island like a goat in a petting zoo."

"That's not the way it was!"

From a man who had compared his sons—and women!—the way a horse breeder spoke of stallions?

"It was. It's adorable you think his interest was his grandchild, but he was getting back at me for marrying Tina against his wishes. Any 'peace' he was exhibiting in his last days was the gloating knowledge of the kick in the shorts he would deliver to me today."

"How is this a kick in the shorts? You didn't want his money."

"I don't." Val's best day ever had been his final one at boarding school, when suspension had finally turned to expulsion. He had told his father to stuff his fortune and had sought out Javiero for a final, *Have it all. You need it more than I do.*

Javiero *had* needed it. His mother's family had been in dire straits, and resolving their issues had fallen on Javiero's young shoulders. But Javiero possessed his own set of faults and one of them was pride. Val had known it would grate on his brother to win by default. It would soil any sense of achievement for him that Val had forfeited.

True to form, Javiero hadn't been able to stand it. He had subsequently rejected Niko's support and clawed his way to the top under his own steam, proving some point that escaped Val, but he had never expended much energy trying to work out what it could be.

"Niko told me once that he regretted how he handled things with your mothers," Kiara said in a conciliatory tone. "He wished he had fought harder for a better relationship with you both."

The top of his head nearly came off, but Val ignored the fresh knife into an old wound.

"If he had wanted a better relationship with us, he shouldn't have used his last act to set us at odds yet again." In the absence of being able to express his disgust at a dead man, he pointed accusingly at Kiara. "And *you* shouldn't have stood by him and kept me in the dark all this time."

"What do you want? An apology? You were *married*. As far as I can tell, you left me in your bed to go propose to your future wife." Her hand flung out with agitation.

"I spoke to her father." He dismissed that with a roll of his shoulder.

"Either way, it was clear you and I didn't have a future." Angry hurt flashed into her expression. "Being paid for my services didn't make me think, *Gee, I bet he can't wait to raise a child with me. I'd better tell him straightaway.* Your mother—"

"Wait. Stop." He held up a hand. "I left you money for the sketch I took."

"Sure. All right." Her jaw was clenched, but offset. She turned away to hide what might have been a frown of insult. Humiliation?

A lurching sensation in his chest pulled a sickening roil from the bottom of his stomach. His conscience was so small he barely wore it at all anymore, but there were some lines he didn't cross. Sex was very much a freely-given-or-not-at-all thing for him.

"You knew I wanted that sketch," he reminded her harshly. "How did my leaving money for it turn into you thinking I was paying you for sex?"

Her face darkened as she flung around to confront him. "I told you I usually got thirty or forty euros. You left me *five hundred*." Her eyes glittered with shame. "For something you probably threw away a week later."

"That's why you didn't take the money? You didn't think you were worth that much?"

He was talking about her work, but a flash of stark vulnerability seemed to hollow out her soul before she crossed her arms and turned back to the window.

"Obviously, I came to regret that," she muttered.

When? Before or after she had become beholden to his father?

He poured the whiskey he'd mostly forgotten, moodily trying to assimilate this new information.

"How much are you getting these days? For your artwork," he clarified when she stiffened.

Silence, then a reluctant, "A few hundred, but they're fully finished oils. The one in the lobby was nearly two thousand, but that was nepotism on Niko's part. Most haven't sold yet. They've gone to my agent for my show."

"At a gallery? Where?"

"Paris. In three weeks." She mentioned the name, watching him for a reaction as he approached with the drinks. "My agent booked it ages ago," she added as she took the glass he offered. "When we thought Niko had more time and before Scarlett— Right." She shifted to set aside her glass. "I can't drink. Scarlett might need me. In fact, I should keep my phone out so I don't miss another call."

* * *

Kiara used the search for her phone as an excuse to put distance between her and Val, still taking in that he hadn't paid her for sex. It was yet another brick in her wall of defenses that had crumbled to powder, leaving her feeling in the wrong, but what choices had been *right* back then?

Her phone was annoyingly empty of notifications, not that she typically had many. On Niko's request, she had closed her social media accounts when she had moved to Greece. Aside from emails from her agent, she typically only exchanged a few texts with Scarlett or the nannies and only when she was too lazy to walk from her studio back into the villa.

"That's a good gallery." Val poured her rejected drink into his own before he took up her spot by the window. "Who's your agent?"

She told him and told herself she was only gazing on his male form as an artist, but seriously, the way his jeans hugged his butt was sublime.

"Dad really came through for you," Val said derisively as he sipped.

She squirmed internally. Niko had, and his leg up contributed to her feeling like a fraud, not that she wanted to hand that weapon to Val.

She looked at the shoes Niko had bought her. She hadn't liked taking all these things. She hadn't felt entitled to live like royalty and had been aware that doing so put her in a beholden state to Niko's implacable wishes.

The studio and agent and standard of living had all been cherries, though. The real draw had been the connection to her child's family. Val had been out of reach and his mother hadn't wanted her grandchild to exist, but Niko had wanted his granddaughter to be part of his life.

Kiara hadn't been able to turn her back on that request, not when she'd spent almost her whole life without any blood ties of her own.

As for Aurelia...

"Sit on your high horse if you like, Val, but when Niko learned I was pregnant, his first reaction was to offer support. Yours was to call me a gold digger and say you didn't want to hear your own child's name. Do you *want* to be a father?" She brought her head up, never comfortable in confrontation, but she refused to be cast as a villain. "Or do you just want to judge me for the choices I've made as a mother? Does all this anger you're spewing have anything to do with me and Aurelia? Or is it actually unresolved issues with a man who is dead?"

Val might have stiffened, but a dark smile of warning crept across his face. "Do you really want to psychoanalyze me, Kiara? You'll be swimming with sea monsters."

"I really want to know." She picked up a cushion and hugged it, running her fingers over the silky tassels, dimly aware of the betraying body language in using it as a shield, hugging it the way Aurelia hugged her bear, but she needed something to bolster her. "Would you like me better if I'd relied on *your* money all this time instead of your father's? Should I have scraped by in low-end jobs to prove that I'm, what? Above needing help? Would noble suffering on my part neutralize your disgust in me?"

"It would be a start." *So* disparaging and sanctimonious.

"Do you know what disgusts me?" She threw the cushion back onto the leather sofa. "That you had the *luxury* of rejecting your father and his money and *did*. Is your mother difficult to live with? Mine's dead. Try hearing *that* at nine years old."

She hadn't meant to reveal that. It was her own very deep, very private anguish, but she refused to be slotted into his pigeonhole of "greedy sycophant."

"I was given a bed in a room with three other girls and a single drawer to hold what I'd been allowed to take from my home. For the rest of my childhood, I wore used clothes from a box that arrived four times a year. I wasn't good in school and I'm terrible at sports. I'm not outgoing, I don't sing well and I didn't put out. The few friends I made were as miserable as I was and moved on as soon as they could, distancing themselves from everything about that life, including me."

He wasn't moving, not even drinking, only watching her as though weighing every word, turning each one over, inspecting it for lies.

"But I had my art." Her voice shook with the emotion she couldn't suppress. "Charcoal doesn't care if you stink like a deep-fat fryer. I worked awful jobs for awful people and lived in squalor and it never mattered because my sketch pad was my door to a better world. When you left me that money, I stared at it for a full thirty minutes before I decided it was a line I couldn't uncross."

"It was for the sketch," he reiterated, swirling his drink before he took a gulp.

"When I found out I was pregnant, I didn't care what you had paid me for," she admitted. "I just wished I'd taken it." She hugged herself as she recalled those bleak days as she had tried to figure out a future that wouldn't result in being labeled an unfit mother. "My life had always been hard. I knew I would plod along one way or another, maybe see what I could get for those sketches I had of you, but your father made me an offer that meant I could give Aurelia the kind of future that would never include bedbugs and pervy landlords. If *I* died, she would always have *something*. Doesn't your daughter deserve to live comfortably? Am I really a villain for giving her the very best start in life that was available to me?"

She was shaking and he was only staring at her with that cynical curl of disdain at the corner of his mouth.

"If you knew how many sob stories and rationalizations I've heard out of my mother in my lifetime," Val drawled, throwing a healthy sting of whiskey into the back of his throat. He was trying to keep himself from swallowing all that she'd said. "The bit about wanting what's best for your child? I've seen that episode more times than I can count."

Kiara sucked in a pained breath as if he had physically struck her. She blinked. Rapidly. She had already been looking shaken enough to make it seem as though relaying the story of her deprived childhood had been difficult. And real. Now her eyes welled.

"I need the ladies' room," she choked.

Val frowned as she rushed away.

Tears were meant to be displayed, to sell him on how hurtful he'd been with his scathing dismissal so he would believe she'd been pouring real heartache onto the floor. That's what his mother would have done.

Something wobbled in his chest as he watched her go, especially when she didn't add an enticing roll of her hips, as some women might, to cloud his head.

He tried to loosen his tie only to discover he wasn't wearing one.

Don't fall for it, he warned himself. She was the enemy. Exactly like the rest of the people he called "family."

Then why had she left the money that night?

He kept coming back to that, especially in light of what she'd said a few minutes ago.

At the time, he'd seen her leaving the money as a charming gesture, as though she had gifted him with the memory of their night by letting him have the sketch without payment.

Of course, he had fully expected her to be compensated once she sold his nudes, but as far as he could tell, she never had. Not even to support their child—although that would likely have revealed to the public her child was his, so he could see why she might have balked.

But that would have allowed her to soak him for support.

I stared at it for a full thirty minutes before I decided it was a line I couldn't uncross.

If she was as mercenary as his mother, and as cold-bloodedly intent on advancing her own interests as his father, why hadn't she taken the money he'd left and why hadn't she come back for more?

She *had* taken money, of course. Later. From his father.

After trying to reach him.

She hadn't reached out to his father. His mother had brought about that alliance.

Why did it bother him so much that she had let herself become reliant on Niko? *Was* he obsessed with gaining the upper hand over a man who was already dead?

If Niko and his fortune had never existed, neither would Val. Maybe the old man's footprints weren't the pair he wished had never trod this earth, Val thought darkly. Maybe he wished his own hadn't.

Kiara came back, not looking at him as she found her clutch. She had washed the makeup off her face. Her hair was damp at her hairline and there were a few water spots on the front of her dress.

"Delightful as this reunion has been," she said in a voice that still held a quaver, "I'll ask the registration desk to find me another hotel." Her hand trembled as she picked up her phone, voice hardening as she added, "And the fact my daughter will have the same ability to walk out on a man trying to cut her down is the reason I will *never* regret taking your father's money."

She leveled him a look that cut past his shields to punch into his gut. It would have been an exit worthy of him if she'd managed it. Her phone buzzed in her hand, though.

Tremendous vulnerability overcame her at whatever she saw on the screen. He instinctively leaped on it as an extraordinary weakness he could exploit.

She arranged a smile on her discomfited face as she swiped. "Hi, baby."

The most joyous, dollish voice he had ever heard said a very exuberant, "Mummy!"

"Are you having fun with Nanny?" Kiara sank onto the sofa, disappearing into the screen the way he'd seen her do once before, when she had opened her sketch pad.

Fascinating.

The voice babbled about "bubberflies" in the garden.

"Did you see Kitty?" Kiara asked.

He couldn't resist. He crossed toward Kiara and she lifted a gaze that held real fear. Her hand tightened on the phone and her whole body tensed.

He stayed out of the camera angle but took in the small oval face on the screen. She had a slightly lighter shade of her mother's brown skin and Kiara's lips. Her corkscrew hair stood around her face like dandelion fluff with sun-tipped ends. She was pointing off screen, telling a story that made no sense, but he could have listened to her earnest chatter for hours.

When she looked back at the screen, he saw pale, silvery eyes, familiar as his own in the mirror. Something heavy landed in his chest. He wanted to apologize to her for tainting her with any shred of himself. She was so damned natural and unbroken and pure.

And even though he knew he had no business soiling her existence with his own, all he could think was, *Give me that child.*

Why? He had never liked children even when he'd been one. They were mean and whiny and most of them were vanity projects on the part of parents who shouldn't have been granted the license to duplicate themselves. He'd been a small adult in the workforce before he'd understood that it wasn't normal to let people take your picture for money.

This child, though? He wanted to reach through the screen and *take* her. Where? And do what? He didn't know, only that he wanted to hold her. Curl his arms around her and ensure nothing impacted the sweetness she wore so artlessly.

"Oh, no, lovey, I'm not in my studio," Kiara

said as a joggled vision of grass appeared. "Remember? I went in the helicopter with Auntie Scarlett. I have to stay here with her. She's having her baby."

The image stopped and righted. Aurelia's face appeared again. "Can I see?"

"Not yet. Soon."

Kiara's smile was so tender, Val found himself rubbing the heel of his hand against his breastbone, trying to ease the sensation of the hard shell around his heart being pried open, leaving breezy cracks and raw spots. Wind whistling into chasms. He had to remind himself to breathe.

"I'll be back in the morning. One more sleep," Kiara assured her.

"No, Mummy." The little girl frowned with dismay. Maybe even distress. "I want you now."

"Oh, baby." Kiara's eyes welled and her smile wobbled.

The nanny stepped in to distract the girl and they quickly said their goodbyes, promising to talk to Mummy at bedtime.

The call ended and Kiara pressed the phone

between her breasts, drawing a breath to gather her composure.

"See?" she said with a falsely cheerful smile. She stood and wiggled the phone. "I don't need any guilt trips from you. I'm on a permanent self-inflicted one, thanks." She threw the phone into her handbag and started for the door.

"Kiara."

Do you want to be a father?

He didn't know what he wanted beyond, "I want my daughter."

CHAPTER THREE

THOSE WORDS WERE her kryptonite. Perhaps she'd given that away when she had mentioned having no family.

She was still shaken by his callous dismissal of the poverty she'd endured most of her life. A poverty both material and emotional.

She shouldn't have been surprised by his behavior. Niko had warned her that Val was contemptuous and judgmental and had learned the fine art of manipulation at the knee of his mother. Even Scarlett had called him "challenging" and "intentionally difficult."

That hadn't been her experience the night she met him, though. He'd been arrogant, yes, demanding she show him the sketches she'd made of him, but he'd then praised her talent and sat for more. Part of her had wondered if he was flattering her to get her into bed, but he'd offered constructive critique and positioned himself in better lighting, sitting patiently while she worked. He had very generously encouraged her to use his notoriety to make a name for herself.

It wasn't until he was married and his mother was so dismissive that she had begun to worry she'd misread him. Then Niko's and Scarlett's reports had further helped her rationalize going along with Niko's wish that she keep Aurelia a secret.

Val had a right to his anger over that, but, "Are you saying you intend to challenge me for her?"

Her heart pulsed as a lump in her throat. She would fight to the death to keep her daughter, but didn't want to put any of them through it.

"I told you, I want to marry you. I want her in my life." He spoke firmly, but his shoulders were tense, his gaze guarded.

"Are you certain?" She wasn't an outwardly

tough person. She had the strength of perseverance, not pushback. When it came to her daughter, however, she was pure mama bear. "Because I would do nearly anything to give Aurelia a good father. And I will do everything in my power to avoid giving her a bad one."

Meeting Val's gaze was such an act of courage every time she tried it. She wasn't nearly as brave as she was pretending to be, but her statement wasn't bravado or warning. It was a heartfelt vow.

Something she couldn't interpret flickered in his silvery-blue eyes. Her daughter had those same steely, piercing irises. She tried not to let the glimpse of her beloved girl in this ruthless man sway her. He already affected her merely by being in the same room.

His cynicism had nearly cut her in two a few minutes ago, but even when he was denigrating her choices and mistrusting her motives, she couldn't stop looking at him. She wanted to sketch him again. Talk in the meandering way they had that night. Like equals.

She wanted to touch him and lie with him and feel his powerful body thrusting into hers.

As that unbidden image entered her mind, a prickling sting climbed from her breasts to her cheeks.

Heat came into his eyes as though he read her mind. A faint smile touched his smooth lips. "Anything?" he mocked softly.

Her heart caught the hiccups and her knees went weak. She yanked her gaze away.

"I—I'm open to letting you meet her," she said, scrambling to recall things she had prepared herself to say when she had believed this conversation would play out in a boardroom where Scarlett and Davin would smoothly step in if she stumbled. "But you have to be sure about your commitment level. I won't bring you into her life only to have you disappear if things don't work out."

"Has that happened?" His tone dropped like an ax. "With other men?"

"Like Niko?" she shot back. "Yes. She wasn't seeing much of him the past few weeks.

He was rarely conscious. She's confused and keeps asking when he's coming back."

Kiara was still struggling with the loss herself. Niko had been in so much pain, it had been a merciful relief when he had finally let go, but everything had changed with his passing.

"You know I mean lovers," Val growled.

She offered him the blithe smile she was learning from him. "I don't feel we're at the stage in our relationship where we can ask about each other's lovers."

"*We* are lovers." The velvety timbre in his voice caressed her ears, swirling heat through her with nothing more than a careless reference to the memories they shared.

"Were," she said in a strangled voice.

"I am a seer of all things, Kiara. Especially human nature." He knocked back the last of his drink and set it aside, then used his gaze to stoke the desire taking hold in her. "You want back into my bed."

Tendrils of culpable desire curled in her abdomen, but she managed to choke, "There's that arrogance I've heard so much about."

Her words were smoke and mirrors, no substance to back up her bravado.

All shreds of humor fell from his expression.

"I see through lies as clearly as you see pictures on a blank page. Look me in the eye and tell me you don't want to have sex with me."

She tried, but she couldn't. Her throat seized up and her gaze dropped to his shoulder then strayed across to the open button where a few fine chest hairs were visible. Her artist's eye began cataloging shades and angles, the strain of fabric on his biceps and the flat bones of his bare wrist. The timeworn softness in his jeans. The missing rivet at his pocket and the ripple of his fly. Denim hugged hard thighs, and swarthy skin peeked through exposed threads above his knee.

She watched his black boots walk toward her until the toe of one halted between her painted toenails. The other caged the side of her right foot.

Heat radiated off him. The embers inside

her glowed red-hot. Sparks seemed to rise around them as if bellows fanned her latent desire into a conflagration.

Her gaze snagged on the sardonic indentation at the corner of his mouth.

"You would prefer a platonic marriage?" His voice had gone sensually rough the way it'd gone when they'd been in bed.

Her mouth pursed to form her answer, but she dimly realized that saying no would be an agreement to marry. He was a very dangerous, crafty man. Infinitely seductive and infinitely sly.

"Hmm?" he prompted. His warm hand cupped her neck.

Her pulse was already thudding. The pressure of his hand against her artery made her heartbeat reverberate in her head.

She couldn't see what was in his eyes. All she saw was his mouth. She could sketch it in her sleep, that full, squared-off bottom lip and the well-defined peaks of the upper lip. Photographs didn't do justice to the smoothness of them. To the way they darkened and sheened when his tongue dampened them.

She wanted that mouth on hers. Ached with three years' worth of yearning to taste him again.

His mouth hardened with savage satisfaction right before he crashed it onto hers.

His lips arrived in one hot sweep that tasted of whiskey and triumph. He pressed and angled in a lazy, confident demand for full possession, taking her simmering desire to an explosive, rolling boil.

She rocked weakly into him, thrust into the depths of passion, the kind she'd only experienced once, and that time there'd been a gradual buildup to get here. The suddenness of pure want that speared into her made her light-headed. Maybe she wasn't even breathing. She didn't care. Thought abandoned her and she opened her mouth wider to welcome his ravaging. To deepen their kiss and greedily take everything he offered, slaking an arid thirst.

His arms closed around her, deliciously hard as he dragged her body into his, sending her mind spinning even more as he squeezed her against his strength. She wanted more.

More heat. More sensations of firm muscle ironed to her front, strong hands molding her back, his sharp scent hitting her brain like a drug.

She ravenously thrust her fingers into the silky strands of his hair. Her other hand went around his neck as she lifted on tiptoe, trying to increase the pressure of their kiss to the point of pain, needing a more acute sensation to appease the depth of longing in her. Needing all of him. Faster.

His tongue sought hers and that wicked intrusion stole the air from her lungs and tightened every inch of her skin. Her nipples hurt and heat rushed so sharply into her loins she groaned at the ache.

With a growl, he slowly ran his big hands from her hips to beneath her butt cheeks and pulled her higher, almost off her feet so the steely shape of him, fully aroused, ground against her mound while his entire body strained tautly against hers.

She hung against him, drowning in sensations, only startled back to awareness when he blatantly sucked on her bottom lip, teeth raking the sensitive inner tissues as he released her and lifted his head.

Now she saw his eyes, narrowed in mockery, but with a feral light that called to her. Taunted but urged. *Lie back. Open for me.*

With her pulse hammering low and hard in the aching place between her thighs, she nearly did. Instead, she protectively folded her top lip over her bottom one, aware now of the tender sting his teeth had left there. Her muscles were weak, her skin sensitized, her libido well and truly returned from whatever maternity leave it had taken.

She dropped her hands to his chest and he very slowly eased his grip on her backside so she could settle onto her unsteady heels. She had to hold his forearms to keep herself upright, still breathless and dizzy. And mortified.

Look me in the eye and tell me you don't want to have sex with me.

She couldn't. Not now. She could fairly smell the grim satisfaction wafting off him and had no way to deny how she'd reacted. She was appalled to realize that if he hadn't called a halt, she might have been on her way to another unexpected pregnancy.

"There are different levels of want," she managed to say. She dropped her hands from his arms and moved away, feeling as though each unsteady step only found dunes of sand.

When she was beyond arm's reach, she turned and pushed her gaze to meet his. It was like thrusting herself into the center of a fire gone silver-white with heat. Her eyes stung and her lungs strained for air, yet she wanted to walk straight back into that inferno.

"Of course I'm attracted to you. Point me to the woman who isn't." Did he think she *liked* being one more in a line he could choose from at random? "I don't *want* to be attracted, though. I don't *want* to act carelessly when I need to forge a mature relationship with the father of my daughter. You look *me* in the eye and tell me I would be your lover in the truest sense of the word. Then we'll talk about whether we'll have sex. Or marry."

She watched his mental retreat as clearly as if he took several steps back himself. The unmistakable rejection stung, but at least she knew exactly what this had been—a lesson. Not reunion or nostalgia or, in her case, indulgence of a lingering crush on a man who had accidentally given her nearly everything she had ever wanted.

She fiddled with her clutch, trying not to betray how skinless his rebuff left her.

"Which hotel is your mother at? I don't want to accidentally bump into her. Actually, I'll sit at the hospital until there's news."

"You'll stay here with me," Val said on reflex.

"No. I won't." Kiara spoke with a quiet dignity that held an underpinning of wariness, maybe hurt. Whatever it was, he understood it to be a concern that he would pressure her for sex.

"There are two bedrooms." As he said it, his libido howled against his efforts to bank it. *That kiss.* He hadn't felt so alive in three years. He wanted more. *Now.*

The fine tremble in her fingers revealed the wild depth of desire still lurking beneath her efforts to pull her composure back into place.

That passion had intrigued him from the first time they met. She came across as a wide-eyed observer on the sidelines of life, but it only took one kiss to tap into the absolute essence of life that teemed within her.

Both then and now, everything had fallen away when she had yanked him into her world of pure, unbridled sensuality. He'd never experienced anything like it with anyone else. It disturbed him.

It seemed to outright terrify her.

While her demand to *tell me I would be your lover in the truest sense of the word* unsettled him.

There were some lines even his pathetic standards of behavior wouldn't cross. He didn't pay for sex, didn't force it and he didn't lie to get it. In fact, his brutal honesty was the core of his reputation as a complete waste of unblemished skin.

While Kiara's brand of truth telling kept jabbing holes into his thick hide.

"It's too early to go for dinner," he noted. "Let's buy you some art supplies." He checked for his wallet and headed to the door.

"Why?" She stayed where she was, frowning with suspicion.

"I'm afraid you'll compromise my virtue if we stay here," he said, not entirely being facetious.

Her flush and the way she tucked her elbows into her sides as though a shiver of excitement accosted her nearly undid him, but he had fallen into bed with her once before and look where they were.

No, he would set the ground rules before they went any further. Did she really believe in love? Because he had hard proof it was a lie sold to children like Santa Claus and the tooth fairy. But they shared a child and they *would* share her.

"I could simply leave. We can take this up another time," she suggested.

She wished.

"You said your sketch pad is your way of coping. You'll relax if you have one in your hands." Perhaps be less inclined to plot or lie.

"Why would you want that? Oh, is this like when a colonel offers a nice meal as a switch-up from torture to get the interrogation victim to trust him?"

"You see straight through me."

"I can't be won over with a sable brush and a prestretched canvas."

"Would you prefer to stay here and hammer out the terms of our marriage?" His phrasing was deliberate, and the way she caught her breath was deeply gratifying.

"I'm getting the feeling my preferences don't matter."

"Smart woman. Shall I look up some shops or—"

"I know where I'm going."

"I thought you might."

The shop owner greeted Kiara like a long-lost daughter, asking if she was on the hunt for something in particular.

"I happened to be in the city and came to browse." She spoke Greek, a language Val could speak fluently, but he preferred his mother tongue of Italian.

The owner urged her to take her time and she began poking through the shelves.

Val wandered behind her, content to observe as she weighed long-handled brushes across her fingers and opened drawers in a supply stand and smelled pastel sticks.

"I lied," she said with a sheepish upward glance through her lashes. "I can be bought with cheap crayons and a paper bag. I am a child in a candy store here and will likely throw a tantrum when you insist it's time to leave."

"Tell me about your show. More important, will I be in it?"

She paused in studying a pane of glass, setting it back with careful attention to its sharp edges. "I've never shared your sketches with anyone."

"No?" The paradox of Kiara was that she seemed truthful but behaved in ways that went directly against the way he expected. That left him wanting to doubt her, but she hadn't seemed to spin or prevaricate her reasons for accepting his father's support. Why would she lie about something else that was quite small in comparison? "Why not?"

She flicked him a glance that snagged a

barbed hook into his chest and hauled him three years back in time to the moment she had straddled his naked thighs. The soft cotton of her skirt had bunched against him as he had dragged her deeper into his lap. Beneath the faint scent of charcoal dust on her hands had been a more earthy fragrance on her skin. Something reminiscent of savory herbs and the damp history imbued on the air of Venice itself. She had smelled of his own country while she tasted of the chocolate and strawberries and wine they had sampled along with an elemental flavor he couldn't name, but had instantly found addictive.

He didn't hide the lascivious memory expanding in his mind. He vividly recalled every caress and moan and pleasured cry they had shared that night. It was a highlight reel he tapped into far more often than all the other kinky fantasies in his self-pleasure vault combined.

A deep flush rose on her cheeks as she met his gaze. He half expected her to turn away, but even though self-consciousness and vulnerability flickered across her expression, she only said, "Niko didn't want our connection made public until after his death. And please don't knock me for this, but..." Her brow crinkled and she tickled her lips with the hairs of a fan brush. "Niko may have provided my supplies, but I did the work. When I sell something, I want people to buy what I've created, not try to acquire the object I've rendered, in this case *you.*"

"That was kind of the point. You didn't lack talent, Kiara, only visibility and resources. That's why I told you to use me."

You'd be the one getting exposure, she'd said with a blushing smile when he'd told her to sell his images.

Today she chewed pensively at the corner of her mouth and dropped the brush into the basket he held for her. "I wasn't sure *I* wanted our connection made public. I mean, if I sold them so I could raise your baby, someone likely would have figured out she was yours. And since those images were all I had of her father, was it right to sell them? It was a quandary."

"You preserved my nude images as a memento for our daughter? I *am* flattered."

"I'm saying there were a lot of complicated factors to consider. Every action had serious repercussions." Her shoulder rolled self-consciously. "Also, our night together was private."

"I don't even know what that word means." His illegitimate birth had been headline news, and the start-up capital of his personal fortune had been earned in his underwear. His bad-boy reputation had been as valuable as his startlingly piercing eyes and perfectly proportioned physique. Even as they spoke, he could tell the shop owner had recognized him and was working up the courage to ask him for a selfie so he could post it and gain some publicity for his store.

Kiara's reaction didn't make sense. She sounded protective of their affair, which suggested their night was special to her in some way. Or shameful?

The back of his throat went gritty and dry at the thought.

"I've tried to paint off them a few times,"

she murmured absently. "In oil and watercolor. Even tried acrylic and pastels. Nothing has ever turned out right. I haven't figured out why." She frowned. "I've had success working off other sketches. I'm pleased with Aurelia's."

She took out her phone, swiped and handed it to him. "Go left and you'll see the rough work. My agent is framing them up and displaying them with the finished painting as a representation of my process."

Even the small image of the painting brimmed with the girl's irrepressible spirit. A half dozen charcoal sketches followed from different angles, all showing her blowing bubbles through a wand. He went back to the oil and expanded the image to see Kiara had caught prisms of light in the soap bubble and the gleam of delight in Aurelia's eyes.

More viscerally, he could sense the pride and joy Kiara felt toward the girl.

"I want all of these." He flicked back to the first sketch of the girl.

The anxious desire for approval in Kiara's expression fell away. She primly took back her phone. "They're not for sale. I won't let anyone acquire *her*, either."

Two hours later they were shown to the best table on a rooftop restaurant overlooking the Acropolis.

The sun wouldn't set for a few hours, but an overhang shaded them and a light breeze came across from the sea in the distance. The city sprawled along that sparkling backdrop and the Parthenon stood in ancient glory against it.

Kiara had been on the verge of panic after their kiss but had relaxed once she'd spent time amongst her most steadfast friends. Strangely, she hadn't felt pressured by Val's presence as she shopped. Aside from the odd, "How do you use that?" he'd allowed her to wander the aisles at her own speed. Talk about a gift!

One that came with a catch. She had tried to put her supplies on her own account, but he had been adamant about covering what had mostly been impulse buys. Now she felt indebted, which had likely been his intention.

Her nerves were creeping back, too, as they moved from her world back into his. She ought to be used to wealth after living with Niko, but despite the fine dining and even finer linens, she hadn't experienced a lot of this lifestyle. She didn't socialize or jet-set or dance at night clubs or sail between islands. She still felt like a guest at Niko's villa, a welcome one, but nothing was hers.

She would be a guest in her daughter's home now, she realized. Or would she?

She glanced uncertainly at Val, and her stomach swooped. He was watching her from beneath hooded eyes. The light threw shadows into his face, accenting his hawkish bone structure.

"You should have brought some of your new toys."

She had left her purchases in the car. "I would only get my hands dirty and not be able to eat. Thank you for indulging me, though." She offered a faltering smile. "Between being a new mother and building my portfolio, then preparing for my show and

Niko's declining health, I haven't had an un-scheduled moment in forever."

In fact, she was feeling very much at loose ends. She glanced at her phone as she set it next to her plate. "Still nothing from Scarlett."

"Why are we waiting around like this?" he asked tersely. "She's a grown woman in the hospital doing something quite natural. Let's get Aurelia and go to Italy."

She blinked in shock. "Are you joking?"

"I'm not saying childbirth sounds easy or fun, but pretty much every female goes through it. There doesn't seem much that any-one else can do while she does."

"Wow. I'm glad I had Scarlett with me rather than you when I delivered. Now I'm genuinely worried she's only got your brother." Was Javiero as absent of compas-sion as Val?

Her words seemed to arrest him. "Did you *want* me there?"

Oops. "Um…" She tried to shrug it off. "A little, I guess."

"Why?" He seemed genuinely astounded.

"Exactly what I'm asking myself right now," she retorted, sipping the water that arrived.

Val declined the wine list and ordered a mixed platter of appetizers.

"Tell me," he commanded when they were alone. "I thought sentiment or morbid curiosity drove a man into the delivery room. What possible use is anyone but a medical professional?"

"Are you kidding me?" Her accent slipped back into Cork, but she could see he was dead serious. "Fine, I'll play." She folded her arms on the edge of the table. "Have you ever been really sick or had a broken bone or been helpless in some way? In a way that made you physically want to step out of your body, but you couldn't?"

Silence crashed down like an iron curtain between them. The frostbite in his gaze jumped so far down her throat, a jolting thud rocked her in her chair. He pinned her with that arctic stare for interminable seconds, impaling her while a panicked tightness clamped around her throat. The oxygen around them evaporated so fast the air sizzled with electric warning, as though a lightning bolt could strike at any second. Her pulse began to pummel her inner ears.

Kiara pushed herself into the back of her chair while she searched his face, trying to discern what she had said to make him that angry, that fast.

His inexplicable rage vanished as swiftly as it had manifested. He transferred his attention to the view, profile inscrutable. "What good would I have been, if that's how you were feeling?"

She took another hasty sip of water, trying to gather her thoughts after that disturbing interchange.

"Well, um, it's terrifying to feel that way," she pointed out and waited to see if he would agree.

Nothing. He was made of granite now, faceless and toneless and immovable.

When she didn't continue, he finally looked at her again, all his emotions banked behind an impenetrable expression. "I couldn't have changed what you were going through."

"No. But… Well, Scarlett held my hand and spoke for me when I couldn't. That meant a lot. The whole process is incredibly undignified. She was a sport about it, but I think a woman who's physically intimate with her partner probably feels less awkward in the moment. When you need an ice chip or a towel, it wouldn't feel so much like you're prevailing. Your partner is as invested in the baby as you are, so I imagine labor feels a little more of a team effort."

She let herself travel inward to those intense hours.

"Scarlett was concerned for Aurelia, of course, but not the way I was. I felt very alone. I couldn't help thinking the only other person who would be as worried for her safe delivery would be her father."

His gaze was unwavering now, not so much holding hers as caught in it. He was hanging on her every word, which perturbed her, making everything she was saying feel even more personal and profound.

"It feels as though it lasts forever and just when I thought I couldn't do it anymore and had to give up, she arrived. They put her on my chest, and she was this ridiculous little tree frog making croaking noises." Her eyes teared up so the sun reflecting off a glass at the end of the rooftop splintered rainbows through her vision.

"Scarlett was thrilled for me, of course, but I thought you might be happy *with* me. Everything I've ever made has been a solo effort, and I've never been more proud of anything in my life, but I needed you to make her happen, and I wanted to show her to you and say, *See what we did*?" She swiped her napkin beneath her damp eyes and warned with a sniff, "If you say something withering or dismissive right now, I will get up and walk away and you will never see her in my lifetime."

He said nothing and she didn't look at him.

Their meze platter arrived, offering her a chance to gather herself back under control while the server spoke to them as though they were tourists. He identified the spanakopita and dolmades, the lamb meatballs and grilled octopus and described the types of cheese and olives and ramekins of tzatziki and hummus and tapenade.

She and Val scooped a few items onto smaller plates.

"*That's* why I'm concerned about Scarlett," Kiara summed up in a voice that still held strains of emotion. "If Javiero isn't giving her the support she needs then I want to."

Val made a noise of disparagement that she took to be an indictment of his brother's ability to be of use to anyone.

"Is that prejudice or should I be worried?" She set down her fork.

"Javiero loves to play the hero. He'll step up."

His cynical statement was hardly reassuring, but Kiara was fairly confident Scarlett would call her if she needed her.

"Are you upset that she's having his baby?" She was curious about the rift between the brothers. How had it gotten so deep? So irrevocable?

"I'm not wishing tragedy on them, if that's what you're asking."

"I didn't think that." Much. "Scarlett likes *your* baby, if that means anything."

"It doesn't," he said flatly. "My feelings toward Scarlett are ambivalent. She did her job for a man I hated. That often meant she was persistent when I wanted her to go away, but better to talk to her than him. I'm not happy she's frightened or in pain, but nor will I experience any happiness when her child arrives. As for Javiero, he does not have the power to affect me in any way. Not anymore."

"Why *did* you hate him? Niko, I mean. And Javiero, I guess."

Val's pensive gaze traversed the horizon, much as it had that afternoon in Venice when he'd appeared in her frame as she made a study of a bridge. She'd been unable to resist sketching him. He ticked all the boxes on classic standards of male beauty, ageless and virile and emanating strength. His skin was smooth over incredible bone structure made up of even, well-defined lines. His strong brow and jaw spoke of power and confidence while his mouth was pure sex and sensuality. His penetrating gaze was observant and intelligent while his stubble and rumpled hair and irreverent remarks ensured the world knew he gave no damns for anyone or anything.

Valentino Casale was very much a man in possession of himself, compelling yet untouchable.

"My father waited until the last possible minute to cut things off with my mother. Granted, a woman with an ounce of pride would have walked away when he told her he was engaged to someone else, but she continued throwing herself at him and he let her."

"Niko told me that she gave up birth control without telling him, hoping to get pregnant before he married Paloma so he would marry her instead. Did she love him?"

"No," he scoffed. "She wanted his money. He wanted a biddable, respectable wife who didn't make public scenes and came with an appropriate pedigree and portfolio of assets. By the time Mother had a positive test to show him, however, he'd applied his best efforts toward making an heir with Paloma. Her pregnancy was confirmed days after they returned from their honeymoon."

"She divorced him when she learned your mother was pregnant, didn't she? Did Niko not consider marrying your mother at that point?"

"Mother expected him to. That's why she went through with having me. But he knew she would lord that advantage over Paloma. No, he decided to recognize us both as his heirs and treat us 'equally.'" He air quoted the word. "He gave my mother exactly what he gave Paloma, a house and an income to support us, which put Paloma's nose out of joint since she would have been entitled to much more if she'd stayed married. How could she, though, amidst such a massive public humiliation?"

"Do you wish Niko had married your mother?"

"I wish he had cut her off cold when he told her he was engaged, rather than continuing to sleep with her. I wish he had paid her off once instead of naming me as Javiero's equal and dangling the promise of any of his money coming to me. I wish he had kept me apart from Javiero instead of sending us to the same boarding school where the legitimate son was placed on a pedestal and the bastard one kicked around like garbage by administration and other children alike. My father should have *picked* Javiero instead of letting our mothers battle incessantly over which one of us was more deserving of his fortune. Javiero was legitimate, but I'm older by two days. Neither woman ever lets the other forget those completely irrelevant details."

Kiara was baffled. "The half that Aurelia stands to inherit is an obscene amount. What on earth is the point in fighting for *all* of it?"

"They were fighting over *him*, Kiara. And he *liked* it. His ego ate up my mother's jealousy and seductions while he was engaged. The squabbles and catfights through his divorce and afterward fed his ego even more. He worked us like fiddles, too, loving those early years when our mothers prodded us to vie to be his favorite. He sent us to school together to prove he was treating us the same, but he compared us all the time. He berated Javiero if I bested him in math. He heckled me if Javiero won the blue ribbon in track and I came second by a hair. I had a sore stomach for three solid years, trying to become what he wanted without knowing what that was. It was hell."

That didn't sound like the Niko she knew, but he'd only had the one grandchild and had thought the sun shone straight out of her.

He'd still seemed angry that his sons had called his bluff and forced him to disinherit them, though. Her impression had been that Niko hadn't known how to bridge the divide, but when she gave it real thought, she recalled his idea of taking responsibility for their rift had always been to say he had allowed Evelina and Paloma too much influence. Kiara had never heard him own up to any particular failures as a father—which, as a parent herself, she knew came with the territory. Her mistakes were pretty much a daily occurrence.

Surely recognizing his own stumbles would have been a first step? Acknowledgment and remorse might have gone a long way with his sons.

"I judged you as spoiled," she admitted. "Earlier, when I said you had the luxury of turning your back on him. That wasn't fair, was it?"

"I gave up on *fair* when I realized what a perverted version of it I was living."

"Is that why you began to rebel?"

"Yes." Cruel satisfaction laced his tone. "My mother had been renting me out to modeling gigs from birth. One day I threw a tantrum. I'd seen her do it a thousand times and I had genuine, pent-up anger. At thirteen, who doesn't? Mostly, I was emulating her, though. It was still an incredible feeling. By acting as though I had lost control, I gained it. Everyone began promising me all sorts of things. I refused to work again until the money I earned went into my own account, not my mother's. She nearly disowned me. Went to my father, of course."

"What did Niko do?"

"He said if I wanted to work, I should work for him. Javiero and I had been dragged into the office every school break for years. That experience taught me the importance of hiring a decent manager and paying attention to what people did with my money, so it wasn't wasted, I suppose. But having my own money allowed me to tell Niko to go to hell. I said the same thing every time we spoke until the night before I met you in Venice."

At which point he had married into the family of Niko's business rivals, firmly building a wall between himself and his father that had never been dismantled.

Kiara knew Scarlett had been in touch with Val a handful of times in the past year, letting him know Niko's health was failing. Val had rebuffed every invitation to visit Niko.

"You don't have any regret that you didn't reconcile with him?" she asked gently.

"None," he confirmed flatly.

"Even though he was not fully to blame? Your mother... I'm sorry, but she seems like she bears some responsibility. How did you maintain a relationship with her all this time, but not him?"

He took a moment to consider his reply, which left her suspecting his answer was incomplete.

"Until today, she believed I was still her golden ticket to at least half of my father's fortune. That kept her on her best behavior. All bets are off now, though, especially once you and I marry. She will become our worst nightmare."

"*And* I could share my daughter with a stranger whom I barely trust? Gosh, how can I resist?"

"You can't. We both speak sarcasm. We're practically soul mates."

His remark was pure mockery, but her heart *thunked* in her chest and sat there reverberating at the thought of finding The One. She took a fresh helping from the platter to hide any secretive yearnings he might glimpse in her eyes. She did sometimes wish for a true, intimate connection with someone, even though—

"Marriage has never been a particular goal of mine," she stated truthfully. "Growing up, I watched the pretty, bubbly girls get attention from boys and wondered what that was like, but the few times I went on a date, I was always waiting for it to be over so I could get back to my sketch pad. That made me realize I wasn't cut out for serious, intimate relationships."

"Is that how you're feeling right now?" he asked drily.

"Is this a date?" A funny tingle curled through her, as if this was the sort of banter a couple might share on a date. A good one.

"If you have to ask, I'll have to try harder." The rakish sweep of his gaze as it struck her lips and throat and breasts was pure, carnal invitation.

She couldn't match his level of nonchalance. Her heart was skipping again so she settled on telling the truth.

"I'm a certified workaholic," she admitted. "I always feel compelled to be making progress with my art if I'm not with Aurelia, but she is my highest priority. That makes this conversation a priority." She swirled a toasted pita bite through some dip. "So this isn't a date. It's a working lunch." Afternoon tea, given the hour, but whatever.

"We're getting married. That usually starts with a date."

And ends with…

She had to fight to swallow her bite of pita.

"I didn't expect you to propose," she said in a small sidestep, rather than confronting his assertion head-on.

"How did you expect me to react?"

"Angry about the money," she admitted honestly. "I thought you'd want to fight for it. It's a lot of money," she added when his expression twisted with annoyed aversion. "Or I thought you would be angry that I'd had her after all and would tell us to have a nice life."

"I am angry. There will be no more keeping secrets from me once we're married. Anything you need, I will provide. My father's money can be dumped in the sea for all I care. This is a clean break from him. Understand?"

So implacable. She didn't dare point out she'd heard an eerily similar command in Niko's tone as he'd extracted her promise to keep Aurelia's existence from Val.

With her eyes on her plate, she said, "Look, it means a lot to me that you want to meet her, but marriage—"

"Kiara," he cut in. "I am the last man to

buckle to convention. Marriage is an idiotic social construct that serves no sensible purpose that I can fathom. But it means something to the rest of the world. Being illegitimate was not fun for me. There were people who made sure I suffered for something that was not my fault. I won't sentence my own child to that experience when it's such an easy fix. Claiming Aurelia as my heir is not enough. You and I have to marry."

Her heart somersaulted. She understood his motives better now. In fact, she felt even guiltier for not telling him about Aurelia sooner. But marriage?

"Is it enough for *you* that she merely knows who I am?" Val challenged softly. "Where was your father when your mother died? Why were you orphaned?"

And here it came. Intellectually, she knew everyone was equal and he was hardly in a place to judge, but that didn't stop others from judging. It didn't stop her from feeling the hollowness of absence.

"I don't know anything about my father," she admitted, locking down her insides so she betrayed no emotion. This was purely a fact about her personal history, she reminded herself. "Maybe my mother would have talked about him once I got older, but she only said he was someone she loved and thought would come back but didn't. After I lost her, I told people I was an orphan so I didn't have to reveal that they hadn't been married. I was never persecuted for it, though."

No, people had expressed pity or maybe puzzlement that it was possible for a person to exist with absolutely *no one* in their life. She'd felt her father's nonexistence in other, subtler ways, though. At times she had thought that at least if she had carried his name, it would have been something. Some tiny connection.

"I could see my way to marrying as a formality, for Aurelia's sake," she allowed carefully. "Perhaps divorce after a year or so?"

"No," he rejected swiftly, cheeks hollow. "I already have one divorce behind me. I didn't think it would bother me, but the stench of failure is intolerable. More important, I don't want to repeat history. I don't want Aurelia torn between warring houses. I won't give you the chance to pit her against me."

"The fact you think I would do that is reason enough we shouldn't marry," she said, spine stiffening. "I don't want to live with someone who doesn't trust or respect me." She let a beat pass, then batted her lashes. "Do you?"

His mouth twitched. He looked off into the distance, faint humor lingering in his profile. "You're entertaining, at least."

"I'm actually very boring. Reclusive. I don't bother with current events or pop culture. I don't care what's trending. If I read, it's romance—not your top pick, I'm guessing. Same goes for movies. My ability to hold court at a dinner party is limited to describing my process, which I hate talking about for fear I'll jinx it. In fact, if you're serious about marriage, brace yourself for two topics of conversation: if the weather supports my plein air aspirations, and how you're coming along with Aurelia's homework, because I had enough trouble at school that I'm calling it right now as your bailiwick."

"Dinner parties are overrated." He lounged easily in his chair, unruffled by her outburst. "Homework I can handle. The talk will be you. I'd suggest anywhere except the dinner table, but I'll leave that up to you. See? Progress. I travel a lot. I assume that appeals. You went to Venice to fill the creative well, didn't you?"

He remembered her saying that? She had been shocked he'd even remembered her name today, let alone the things they'd talked about.

"If my showing goes well, I'll need fresh inspiration," she said, tentatively letting herself consider what marriage to him might look like. "I suppose we could travel with you until Aurelia starts school."

"What difference will that make? She'll be at boarding school."

"You're adorable when you're wrong." She stabbed a meatball, but paused to see how he reacted, prepared to fight to the death on this one. "Aurelia will attend day school. I haven't decided where."

"You're sexy when you're aggressive." He

stole her fork and ate the meatball off the tines, chewed and swallowed. "Which I like. And you know that."

Ride me. Kiara had known how sex worked in a theoretical sense, but she hadn't realized she could take charge of the act and revel in having all the control.

A rush of sensual heat arrived with the memory of undulating on him while the bed creaked. They had already made love twice by then and her body had been tender, but her growing confidence had had her nipping at him. Squeezing him. Pleading, *Once more,* until he'd dragged her atop him.

Ride me, he had urged. *So I don't hurt you.*

She had nearly killed both of them, determined to wring every last ounce of pleasure from the experience. When she had come down from the profound fulfillment that had swept over both of them, she'd been sprawled weakly across him, their heartbeats—

"What's on your mind, darling?" he asked in a tone of exaggerated intimacy.

He knew exactly where her thoughts had

gone. He'd sent her there on purpose, probably to disarm her after she'd asserted herself.

Her flush of sensual tingles turned to a stinging heat of mortification.

"Why was I even there that night?" The question had haunted her for three years. "Online it says you hated modeling and quit as soon as you had capital to pursue other things." Green energy and tech initially, but these days he had fingers in pies from hotels to broadcasting. "Why did you offer to sit for me?"

"I wanted you to come to my room," he said as if that was obvious.

"But *why*? Because even when I thought you'd paid me for sex, it didn't make sense that you would ask *me*. There were far more experienced professionals if that's what you wanted, and fine." She held up a hand. "That's not what it was, but the sort of women you're usually seen with are CEOs and socialites, not impoverished art students with zero sophistication and a stone's worth of excess weight."

"Which one of us are you insulting?" He angled his head in forewarning.

"I know what I am, Val. I didn't like being an ugly duckling as a child, but I'm fine with turning into a plain duck as a woman, not a graceful swan—which *is* your usual type. There were women flirting with you in the restaurant that night so why take *me* back to your room? Was it the thrill of picking up a virgin?"

"What?" The crack of his voice was loud enough to turn heads at the tables that had begun filling up. He gave an annoyed glance around, then asked her more quietly, but with equal intensity, "How the hell was I supposed to know that?"

"I thought it was dead obvious." Granted, the act hadn't really hurt. She'd been incredibly aroused, and the sting of penetration had been more a moment of heightened stimulation than anything else.

"You were on the pill," he reminded under his breath. "That led me to believe— Are you being straight with me right now?"

She shrugged. "Why would I lie?"

"I don't *know*," he growled and rose to throw down some bills. "We're not continuing this discussion here."

"Can we go to the hospital?"

"So Javiero and I can compare notes on how we wound up in the same situation? *No*."

"There's a park next to it. It's nice this time of day. Quiet. I really want to check in on Scarlett."

He relented and ten minutes later his driver let them out to walk through wrought iron gates into a small sanctuary where families could wheel relatives for a breath of fresh air.

The area was abandoned at the moment since the shadow of the building had moved, but there were still a few patches of shade beneath some trees, and a light breeze picked up the mist off the fountain, offering respite from the heat of the sinking sun.

Kiára had come here at different times with Niko but didn't have a tiny hand clinging to her fingers today while little feet walked the rim of the pool. She felt bereft without her girl and gave a sigh of melancholy as she watched water overflow the center vase and fall in a curtain around it.

"Did you—" he began, then ran his hand down his face. His voice tightened as he tried again. "When I invited you to my room and made it clear I would undress, I interpreted that to mean you were up for more than modeling. I said we would see where the rest of the night took us."

"I knew what I was signing up for." She ducked her head with awkward shyness. "I wasn't *that* inexperienced."

"But you let me seduce you, even though you'd never made love before. Why?" He was back to suspicion, not that she'd imagined she had won him over in any way, but the wall of hostility had returned to his expression and made her heart dip.

"I was flattered," she admitted baldly. "I don't get attention from handsome, sexy men and—"

"Stop talking about yourself like you're not attractive."

She closed her eyes. "*Please* don't think I'm fishing for reassurance. I am genuinely happy with looking average and normal. I like food and see no point in sweating at the gym when I'd rather be painting. The life of a supermodel seems vastly overrated."

"It is," he said flatly. "Most thin people I know have eating disorders. My mother is a raving lunatic because she's in a constant low blood sugar psychosis."

"And you?" She opened her eyes wide with false innocence. "Is this charm you exhibit natural or is there a similar underlying issue?"

He dipped his chin and glowered a silent warning.

This was why she used a canvas as a shield against life. Even when she did try to stand up for herself, she wound up getting knocked into the dirt with a wordless glance.

"I do hate modeling," he stated. "When I realized you were sketching me, I assumed you knew who I was and almost walked away, but your intensity made me curious. I wanted to see how it turned out, so I asked you to dinner."

Actually, after standing motionless for twenty minutes, he had walked over and said,

Models are entitled to compensation. Buy me dinner.

He had wound up paying, thankfully, because he had chosen one of those expensive outdoor cafés where they charged more for the table than the food.

His gaze drifted over her features the way it had that night, in a way that made things shift inside her, so she felt very feminine and shy. Pretty and aware. *Sexy.*

"You should have told me you'd never made love."

"Would you still have wanted to?"

"Yes." His response was so unapologetic, she choked on a laugh. "But not *three times.* Did I hurt you?"

Childbirth hadn't exactly been a picnic, but that wasn't what he meant.

"A little. I mean…" She wrinkled her nose and looked toward the fountain, cheeks stinging with self-consciousness. "Can we settle on, it was a perfectly nice experience until I thought you had paid me for it?"

"Perfectly nice," he drawled. "Two words that have never been applied to me."

This was the man who had made her laugh and feel talented and more exciting than she had ever aspired to be. He stole her breath, this gleaming god of a man, tall and wide-shouldered, virile and angular and watching her with a knowing smirk.

"This, Kiara." His voice became graveled and intimate, swirling a buzzing heat through her like the richest red wine. For one second she felt as though they were perfectly aligned. Equal and opposite. Yin and yang. "*This* is why I asked you to my room that night."

"What is it?" she asked with bewilderment. *Soul mates*, she wondered with a depth of yearning so sharp it stole her breath.

"Chemistry," he said, snapping their connection as he frowned. "Have you had other lovers?" His tone suggested he already knew the answer and didn't like it.

She folded her arms and lined her toes up with a seam in the paving stones beneath her feet. "I haven't had time to set up my online dating profile."

Thunderstruck silence followed, then, "So me. That night. That's all the experience you have. And today you kissed me like—" He waved off in the direction of his hotel then took two steps away and turned his back on her. One hand hung off his hip, the other squeezed the back of his neck. "A decent man would not take advantage of you by seducing you again. I am not a decent man, Kiara. You know that, don't you? I will use this attraction to get you into my bed, put a ring on it and that will be the end of it."

He sounded like one of those cartoon villains who revealed his dastardly plan so the hero was forewarned and forearmed, but there was a part of Kiara that didn't want to fight him. The primal female in her was darkly excited by the threat of being dragged to a cave by the male who claimed her.

That ancient imperative to submit had a purpose, however; one that was as clear today as it had been then.

"Can I ask you a related question?"

He looked over his shoulder.

"Do you want more children?"

"No."

It was such a swift punch; she caught her breath.

He turned and frowned. "You do?"

She nodded jerkily. "I hated being an only child."

"Siblings aren't all they're cracked up to be."

"You were poisoned from an early age against one another." She took a step forward, anxious to persuade. "Have you even given Javiero a chance lately?"

"No," he scoffed. "And I won't."

She shook her head in bafflement while her heart felt pulled and strained between him and Aurelia, the past and the future, her own will and his.

"That sort of hatred is not what I want Aurelia to learn."

His jaw tightened. "That is why I won't have another one," he shot back with a forceful point of his finger. "You're already using her to manipulate me."

"Into doing what?" she cried. "Reconciling with your brother? That's between you and him. Do it or don't. I don't care. But my job as a parent is to teach Aurelia how to be a decent human being. To model behavior like kindness and forgiveness. If you're only going to show her how to hate, then no. You don't get to be her parent."

A muscle in his cheek ticked.

Remorse gripped her. She felt as though she was kicking a dog for being a dog.

"Do you understand that being a father is more than giving her a name and a bedroom and three square meals?" she asked more gently. Maybe she even spoke with tendrils of pity because her life might have been a lonely struggle, but his had clearly been a Siberian wasteland.

"This isn't an ultimatum, Val. It's a *choice*. One *you* have to make. If you want me to marry you, you have to also want a relationship with Aurelia. You can't let her form an emotional attachment that isn't reciprocated. That's cruel. *You know that*. She needs all the compassion and respect and affection you can pour over her. You'll have to listen and compromise. That's what was lacking between you and Niko, wasn't it? That's why you're so bitter and malevolent. Do you really expect me to set her up to become just like you?"

CHAPTER FOUR

WALK AWAY, VAL THOUGHT.

But Kiara did it first, saying, "I'm going to check on Scarlett."

He had instructed his driver to park at the hospital, which was the direction she took, but he stayed where he was, staring at one of the handful of shiny coins in the bottom of the fountain.

Did he feel manipulated? Yes. Aurelia had already become a pressure point and he hated giving anyone leverage over him. He'd been weak and manipulated and exploited as a child. Objectified and controlled, lied to and lied *about*. He'd been abandoned by Niko when he had most needed him to stand up for him.

So yes, he was bitter and malevolent. Mostly, he compartmentalized and got on with life, but he had made a habit of caring very little about anything. The minute he cared for more than money or his immediate comfort, he opened himself up to being used and cornered and crushed.

But he already cared about his daughter. He didn't understand the powerful force that had risen in him at the sound of her voice, but something instinctive within him wanted to protect his child in every possible way, most especially from the bullies and predators he'd experienced in his own youth.

Of course, his mere presence in her life would expose her to the tainted world he came from so the best way to protect her was to *walk away.*

His feet refused to budge.

Why not? Kiara had the means to take excellent care of Aurelia. She was proving fierce enough to stand up to him, wasn't she? A savage excitement swelled in him, witnessing how glorious she was in her desire to slay dragons for their daughter.

Then there was their kiss. Their sexual compatibility hadn't faded one iota. Her fire and simple truth drew him as inexorably as the night they'd met.

Do you really expect me to set her up to become just like you?

He pushed the heels of his hands into his eye sockets, convinced he was too far gone to become the better man his daughter deserved.

But he couldn't bring himself to walk away.

Prepared to wait, Kiara detoured to the car to collect a pad and some graphite pencils.

After a brief inquiry with the main desk clerk who promised to make a call to the maternity ward, she settled into a corner of the waiting room and looked for something benign to draw. There were a handful of people here, an elderly couple and a woman with a child absorbed in screen time. There was a potted plant in the corner and a small courtyard beyond the window, but nothing inspired her.

Her mind was brimming with Val and all the fresh angles and expressions he had revealed in the hours she'd been with him. His blade-like cheekbones and the inimical set of his jaw, the sensual sweep of his mouth and the spiky lashes around his pale, steely eyes.

Her own eyes were damp, her throat tight.

She felt so stupid for hoping. No. Robbed. Somehow, deep down, she had convinced herself Niko and Scarlett were wrong. It wasn't as if Val went around murdering people or committing high treason. Sure, he was given to making scathing remarks and pulling ruthless business moves, but he wasn't a bad person. Was he?

She wanted—needed—to believe he possessed a heart and was capable of offering it to his daughter and yes, she was chagrined to admit, to her, too.

She understood now, though. He was broken. He was all ropy scar tissue, no flexible tendons or muscles capable of stretch. He was contemptuous of humanity and lacking in compassion. It was sad. What the man needed was some unconditional love and if she didn't have Aurelia's trusting heart to protect, she might have taken a chance on him.

But she had to put Aurelia first.

Oh, shoot. Her pencil had absently begun

blocking in his naked shoulders, about to re-create the moment when he had turned his head and asked with throaty seduction, *Would you like to make love?*

Her heart had flipped over. She had already been doing so in her mind. The compulsion to caress him with more than her eyes had been impossible to resist.

Her defenses were still as easily breached by him. Was it purely her inexperience? Or that chemistry he'd alluded to? She hadn't known what to think of that. He was a highly sexed man; that wasn't up for debate. She was not a highly sexed woman. Unless she was around him, apparently, because he turned her into some kind of nymphomaniac.

Cheeks stinging, she glanced around as she surreptitiously flipped her page to hide what she'd begun to sketch.

The sound of the entrance doors sliding open lifted her head.

Val entered. His gaze found her, and her heart leaped at the sight of him.

Don't hope, she cautioned herself, but what

did his arrival mean? What did that grave expression mean?

Into the charged silence, the distant ding of an elevator sounded.

Before he even looked in that direction, Val stiffened like an animal going on alert.

Footsteps approached. She couldn't see who it was, but Val turned his head, his expression hardening to iron. He was bristling like a wolf and it made all the fine hairs on her body stand up with trepidation.

Instinct had her rising against a cloud of such dark animosity; the elderly couple sensed it and frowned with concern as she moved past them.

Javiero. She'd seen photos of his rugged features before the attack, but her heart bottomed out when she saw him in person. He was a little taller and broader than Val and wore a black eye patch. Savage red lines stood livid on his face and across his throat. His haggard expression was as rigid as Val's.

They held an unblinking stare, a pair of territorial beasts primed to rip out each other's throats at one false move from the other.

She made herself ignore Javiero's disfigurement and forced a friendly smile.

"Javiero. It's nice to meet you. I'm Kiara."

She tried to put out her hand to shake, but Val swept his arm in front of her, catching her wrist and wrangling her behind him, all without breaking eye contact with his brother.

"For heaven's sake," she muttered, struggling against his tense hold. "He's not going to eat me."

"No comment?" Javiero taunted Val, completely ignoring Kiara. "Not going to say you like what I've done with my hair or something equally banal?"

Antagonism simmered off Val in waves. She fairly tasted it. How could she not? He had his arm bent to wrap around her and she could hear his teeth grinding together.

She gave up trying to twist away and peered around his shoulder. "How is Scarlett?"

"Sleeping."

"She delivered? Boy or girl?" she asked with excitement.

"Boy." Javiero was still holding a macho staring contest with Val.

"How lovely! Congratulations." She pinched Val, trying to get him to ease his grip on her. "Everything went well? No complications?"

"None."

These men! She leaned into Val, trying to nudge him off balance to break their stare, but he was a concrete wall. "Have you chosen a name?"

"No."

"I'd love to see him," she said wistfully.

"No." Javiero seemed to enjoy rounding out the word. His brows lifted ever so slightly in a signal that he was refusing purely out of spite toward Val.

Somehow Val grew harder and larger, his muscles seeming to gather for attack, threatening to tear through the constraints of his shirt, but all he said was a gritty-voiced, "I'll stay here. Let her up."

"No." The satisfaction that dripped from Javiero's tongue should have left a puddle on the floor.

Val's body bunched further.

Kiara wrapped her arms fully around him and squeezed with all her might.

"It's fine," she declared firmly. Strenuously. Even though Javiero's refusal fractured her heart. "It's late." It wasn't, but she would defuse this any way she could. "I'm sure you all want to rest. Please give Scarlett and your son my love. Tell her to call me when she's up for a chat," she babbled.

Javiero didn't promise to relay any messages. He pivoted and stalked away.

The press of Kiara's curves against him eased, but Val had to consciously tell himself to release her. His heart was slamming in his chest, adrenaline leaving an ache in his muscles.

She expelled a hissing breath of pent-up tension. "I'll get my things."

He watched her return to her seat and collect her pad and pencils and followed her out.

He should have walked away instead of coming after her. What had he thought to accomplish? He had only known he was still determined to marry her, not expecting an immediate test of his resolve.

For all his claims that Javiero had no effect on him, the sight of his half brother had clashed old anger through him—after the unsightly, stitched-up tears in Javiero's face had briefly taken him aback. The damage was more extensive than reported, but Val knew better than to pity Javiero. He was still the arrogant hard-ass Val preferred not to know.

And after all the times Val had knocked over Javiero's attempts to claim authority over him, today he'd had to stand there and suffer it. Javiero's refusal to let Kiara see his baby had been pure malice. It had been an attempt to dig at Val and it had *worked.*

Val was incensed to learn he had a crack in his armor, one that Kiara had caused and that Javiero had found quickly and easily. How? It wasn't as if Val had *wanted* Kiara to go anywhere with him. Javiero had talked more than one ally into changing sides in the past. It was one of the reasons Val rarely trusted anyone anymore.

But Kiara's confession earlier about wanting him with her when she had delivered was still panging uncomfortably in his chest. Given her concern all day for her friend, he understood that reassuring herself Scarlett and the baby had come through the ordeal meant a lot to her.

So there he'd stood, helpless to force Javiero into giving him something he didn't even want. This was why he hated Greece! There were never any good choices, only lousy and worse.

"What's wrong?" Kiara asked, coming around from stowing her pad with the rest of her supplies. Her brows came together as she noticed Val's tense fist braced on the roof of the car.

"Scarlett doesn't need you. We can leave." He opened the car door.

"But—"

"He won't let you see her, Kiara. We're getting Aurelia, going to Italy and getting married."

"I haven't agreed to that!" Kiara's eyes widened in anxious uncertainty. Her gaze went back and forth between his eyes as she searched for an answer of some kind.

She didn't have to repeat the question. He heard it loud and clear.

Do you really expect me to set her up to become just like you?

"I didn't finish what the jaguar started, did I?" He had nearly bitten clean through his tongue for her sake, even though he'd been provoked. "*I* wasn't the one being petty, refusing to let you see your friend and her baby. I take your point about Aurelia's confusion over losing Niko. I'm completely committed."

Her breath left her, but still she hesitated to duck into the car.

He knew what she was waiting for—his agreement to develop a bond with their daughter. To be a better father than his own. When the bar had been set that low, how hard could it be?

"I will *try*, Kiara," he promised through his teeth while a band tightened around his chest. "That is more compromise than anyone has squeezed out of me in years. Accept it as the triumph it is."

Kiara didn't feel as though she was winning anything. In fact, she was losing what little autonomy she still possessed.

She had known her life would change with Niko's death. She had known Val would be informed and she would have to handle his reaction.

Knowing hadn't prepared her. Maybe she spent too much time hiding from the real world in her art, making the anguish of daily life easier to bear by painting over it with bright colors and clean lines. That tactic left her with few coping strategies when reality crashed in. She wanted to believe she was strong inside, but she wasn't. She leaned on Scarlett *all the time.* And Scarlett wasn't here. Would she see her again? She'd already lost Niko. Now she would lose her home and her best friend?

What was the alternative, though? She could pick a fight with Val and maybe come out on top after a long, bloody battle, but that would serve no one, least of all Aurelia. If Val was willing to make a concession for their daughter, Kiara ought to, as well, right?

Even if it terrified her?

She kept herself together until they returned to the hotel where she took refuge in the guest bedroom to "freshen up." Instead, she threw herself facedown on the bed, trying not to scream with hysteria into a down-filled pillow.

Twice. She had met Val *twice*, and he had completely overturned her life each time, this time even faster and more completely than the first. What did that say about how marriage to him would go? She couldn't do it. Couldn't.

But she wanted to. Which scared the hell out of her.

A knock sounded and Val's rumbling voice had her scrambling to sit up.

"What?" she stammered.

He opened the door. "I said—"

Her turmoil must have been clear in her flushed, disheveled appearance. His steely gaze flicked to every corner. "What's wrong?"

"What's right?" she choked out as she scooted herself to the edge of the bed and grabbed a tissue. Two. Three. She felt like crying if only to release the pressure inside her. "The closest thing I've had to a father died two days ago. My best friend had a baby that I'm not allowed to see. Maybe I'll never get to talk to her again. *You* expect me to move to a strange country as if it's as easy as rolling over in bed. Would I even have a studio? Because the culmination of my life-time's aspiration is happening in three weeks and I'm not ready!"

If she lost *that*… Cripes. Now the tears were really pressing up against her composure.

"It's a lot to process," she muttered, shoving panic to the edges of her consciousness as she moved to the mirror. Good grief. Her face was ashen, her hair squashed.

"Of course you'll have a studio," he said behind her.

She flung around. "Really? Because it is an absolute deal breaker for me."

He gave her a smirk that could only be described as patronizing. "I don't claim to be an inventive man, Kiara. If my father was able to bribe you with four walls and a roof, why wouldn't I use the same incentive?"

Lord, she was predictable. And easy. "Where?" she asked.

"There's a space on the grounds of my villa that should be big enough. Design whatever you like."

"Really?" She couldn't help a skip of excitement at the idea. She loved her studio on the island, but there were things she would do differently if starting from scratch.

"Of course. I want my wife to be happy."

For some reason, she found that incredibly laughable and she chuckled.

"Why is that funny?" His eyes narrowed.

"I don't know." She sobered. "I appreciate that you want to indulge me, but..." She sighed. "Much as I dream we could become a family for Aurelia's sake, I can't agree to marry you. Not until I have a better sense that you and I will be able to make a proper go of it."

"You make a proper go of it by going all in," he said in a hard voice. "By making a commitment and sticking to it through thick or thin."

"It's just that easy, is it? You're going *all in*? Not going to hold anything back?"

She watched his cheek tick. She wasn't sure

why that went straight into her heart like a branding iron, but it did. She gripped her elbows.

"I'm willing to bring Aurelia to Italy and see how it goes. That's as much as I'll give you right now."

His turn to offer a harsh chuckle that scraped along her nerve endings.

"Take as long as you like to think it over," he said in a mild tone belied by his granite posture and ruthless smile. "So long as you've decided to marry me when our wedding date rolls around in fourteen days. I came in to say you should call the villa, tell them I'm sending my pilot to collect Aurelia. He'll come back for us and we'll proceed to Italy from here."

"What? *No*." Her blood zinged with alarm. "I can't leave from here. I have things I need. From my studio."

"Make a list. Someone can pack and forward it."

"No." Her arms shot straight down at her sides. "No one goes into my studio. Not unless I'm there and invite them. No one touches

my things." The idea made her hyperventilate on a good day. Today she was already over-wrought and bordering on mania.

With a weary sigh, he said, "Tantrums don't work on me, Kiara."

"I'm not joking!" Her arm flailed. "I get up-tight when someone comes in and I'm *there*. People can't go in and touch my *things*."

He caught her wrist and studied the way her fingers were trembling. His touch shifted so he could feel the unsteady race of her pulse.

"They're only things, Kiara," he said quietly.

"They're *my* things and we're going to need a safe word if you're going to make outland-ish suggestions like telling me to let others touch them." She pulled away from his touch, embarrassed and trying to turn her reaction into a joke but failing spectacularly. "I know it's not rational." Her eyes were welling with helplessness. "But my studio is where I'm... *me*." Where she allowed herself to be vul-nerable. "You don't let strangers walk up and touch everything under your clothes, do you?"

He quirked a brow. "Wrong man to ask. I strip for strangers all the time."

Not all the time. Not anymore. Did he? What would happen if they were married? Would he have other lovers besides her?

She hadn't let herself think about sex. About what she might gain with this marriage—like *him*.

Now her pulse tripped into a different kind of gallop. Still fearful, but anticipatory. He was a force, this man. He would never, ever be easy.

But all he had to do was touch her and she melted.

"*No* has always worked for me." He touched her arm again, his touch light and the suggestion of invitation that she come closer even lighter. "As a safe word."

She would never be safe with him.

She knew that without a doubt. She might have money, but he would always have the advantage of experience and control and less personal investment. Wasn't that the definition of her life, though? Whether it was Niko's power or her agent's assessment of her talent or simply her daughter's best interest, Kiara was forever giving or forgiving, allowing or enduring.

Except when it came to sex with Val. Tension was crawling across his cheekbones, some of it sexual, some of it dismay. He was reacting as inexorably as she was, and she didn't think there could have been a stronger aphrodisiac. She might be helpless to the way he made her feel, but he suffered a similar reaction.

She was pretty sure.

Her instinct for creative discovery took over, governing her as she stepped forward. It was the same compulsion that gripped her when she was deep in the throes of painting, when something unexpected happened, but wasn't a mistake.

This might be. She saw Val's gaze dip to her mouth, saw the sway in him the way a redwood rocked in the wind, trying to withstand a force that could topple it.

Yearning curled with eagerness in her belly as she waited.

With a soft curse, he dropped his head and

covered her lips with his, releasing a pained noise into her mouth as he did it.

A moan left her at the same time, one that was both a signal of welcome and a noise of agony at the intense sensation of lips scraping hers. A damp lick—hers—and the friction became a glide. Heat expanded down her throat and across her chest, prickling her nipples to life. Her hand found his stubbled cheek and encouraged him even as his arms wrapped around her and locked her into a tight embrace that squeezed the air from her lungs.

His kiss was devastating. His hand cradled the back of her head, fingers massaging through her hair while he worshipped her mouth. He made love to it so blatantly, a flash flood of heat went straight to her loins. Her knees weakened and she clung all the tighter to him, hips tilting forward, seeking the pressure of him where she ached.

He dragged his head up and his unsteady breaths moved his chest against hers as he walked her backward to the bed.

"Are you going to say it?" he growled.

"What?" She stumbled over her own feet, grasping at his arms to keep her balance.

"Our safe word."

Her tongue went to the space behind her front teeth. Realization struck with a pang of helpless humor along with confusion and a rather tender, frightening feeling because as unwise as this was, it felt incredibly *right*. A quivery, joyous sensation had lodged itself somewhere between her heart and her stomach.

"I'm taking everything," he warned. "Unless you say it."

"Me?" she asked, sinking onto the edge of the mattress because her knees wouldn't hold her. Her agonized gaze pinning to the spot in his throat where his carotid artery pulsed, confident and strong. "Why? To prove I can't resist you?"

"To prove I can still make you scream."

A squeaking sob escaped her, and she continued to hold his arm as he slowly began releasing the tiny buttons that closed the front of her dress.

She wanted him to kiss her again, blank out

her mind so her surrender wasn't so blatant, but he was giving her every chance to voice that tiny word she couldn't seem to find because now his hand was invading. Sliding with surety into her dress, under the cup of her bra, gathering the abundant swell of her breast and baring it.

Another growling noise escaped him, and he overwhelmed her then, pressing her back as he took her brown nipple into his mouth, wet and hot and ruthless.

He caused such a spear of pleasure into her loins; she bucked her hips against his weight.

He shifted, still pinning her, but drawing up the hem of her dress and dancing abstract patterns across her inner thighs until she was squeezing them together to try to ease the growing ache between them.

"This is happening too fast," she gasped, clasping his head.

"Is it?" His voice sounded drugged and his eyelids were heavy as he raised his head. His hand stilled on her upper thigh. The branding heat of it made her intimate flesh throb. "I can smell how excited you are, Kiara."

The tip of his nose circled hers and his erotic words against her lips sent a shower of tingles through her. The line of his own arousal dug into her hip.

"You don't want my touch here?" His thumb skimmed ever so briefly against the line of her panties, causing a fresh release of dampening readiness into her aching folds. "My mouth?"

He grazed his lips against hers, teasing, not giving her the kiss her parted mouth craved, only the flick of the tip of his tongue.

"Tell me what you want," he said with dark command. "Say it and I will give it to you. I promise. I won't make you beg. This time," he added with a carnal smile.

Heaven help her, she did. She said something earthy and flagrant. He revealed his teeth in a wolfish, predatory smile, but in the next second smothered her with a kiss. Then he did as she'd asked, giving her his mouth all over her body, working his way down, exposing her other breast and lifting her skirt high enough to lick into her navel. Then he peeled away her panties and kissed the flesh he'd exposed.

He made her scream.

Then he said, "Louder," and did it again.

"What are you doing?" Kiara's voice was heavy with lassitude as he picked her up.

"I need a condom." If he didn't get inside her in the next sixty seconds he was going to go out of his mind.

"I'm too heavy."

"Don't insult me." He shouldered into his own room and set her on his bed, rather enamored with the way her disheveled clothing exposed a shoulder and a breast. Her skirt rode up and the wrinkled silk told its own story. Her crushed hair and swollen eyelids made him want to push her knees apart and feast on her all over again.

He wrenched his shirt off then slowed as her gaze heated with lust. He popped the button on his jeans and lowered the zipper with care since he was aroused and, as always, commando.

She drew in a breath as he revealed that

fact, gaze pinned to the flesh that was aching to thrust into the heat he'd tasted.

When she licked her lips and stared at him with unabashed craving, he had to squeeze himself to keep from losing control. A pang of pleasure-pain throbbed into the tip, warning him how close he was, but he couldn't resist asking, "Want this?"

She swallowed and her eyes came up to his, her gaze full of vulnerability as she nodded.

This woman would be his undoing, he feared, but he moved closer and let her take him in her too-gentle grip. She was as tentative as she'd been that first night, but the caress of her tongue and the close of her lips and the light suction she applied was pure paradise.

He withstood it as long as he could, fists gripped onto her shoulders, weight pushing into his toes while his abs pulled into his spine.

Everything in him wanted to capitulate to her delicate torment, but he made himself press her back. *He* was in charge. Wasn't he?

"*Grazie, bella*, but take off your clothes,"

he said, barely recognizing his own voice, coming from such a deep place inside him. "I want all of you."

He helped, skimming his fingers across her soft shoulders, bringing her to her feet again so her dress fell off her hips and onto the floor. She released her bra and it dropped away, too.

He feasted his gaze on every inch of her brown curves. The musky scent of sex was all around them and he started to reach for her, then remembered he needed a condom. He picked up his jeans for his wallet.

"I'm, um, still on the pill," she said very softly. "A proper kind. But it's okay if you want to use one," she said as she watched him apply the latex. "To be sure."

He did want to be sure, but as he pressed her onto the mattress beneath him, he wasn't sure of anything anymore.

CHAPTER FIVE

THIS WAS HOW it had been that other time, Kiara thought distantly. The thrust of his body into hers stung, but she gloried in the sensation. In the sheer possessiveness of his action. In the power of his undulating form beneath her hands as they roamed over his back and hips and flexing butt.

Her senses were overloaded, but she loved it. And the pleasure, the abject joy that filled her as they writhed in the throes of lovemaking, was incomparable. It was raw and intimate and her defenses were nonexistent, but she had never felt more free. She released all the constraints within her, at one with him in a way she had never experienced with anyone in any other way except like this, with him.

Orgasm peaked sudden and sharp in her, pushing a cry of surprise from her throat.

He laughed and speared his hand into her hair, not pausing his rhythm as he nipped at her jaw.

"We can do better than that. I want you to *weep*, it's so good." He dragged her hands over her head and stretched her helpless beneath him while his busy mouth traversed dips and curves, finding all her erogenous zones, making her groan under the onslaught of pleasure.

Climax rose again, stronger. The next one was stronger still.

She said things then, things that were pleas for mercy and entreaties for more. She forgot everything she was. The only thing that mattered was the man who commanded her here, in this bed. She was his, utterly and completely his.

It should have terrified her.

And it did, later, when she came back to herself and realized how much power he had over her. But for now, she exulted in it.

"I hate the island," Val said forcefully, hours later, when they had emerged from his room, sleepy and famished, to order room service and circle back to the discussion that had preceded Kiara's forging herself onto him like iron filings to a magnet.

Kiara looked up from folding back the sleeve on her robe, shocked by the vehemence in his tone.

"*Hate* it," he reiterated. "I didn't go back when my own father was dying there. What makes you think I'll go back tomorrow?"

"Your daughter?"

"My daughter can come to me. *You* want to go back. Why? Your studio?" He made it sound like a very lame excuse.

"Yes." A deep quavering accosted her as she watched his eyes narrow the way a cat's did when a bird landed nearby. If he'd had a tail, it would have flicked with predatory anticipation. "I can go alone," she said, scooping saffron-flavored rice into her mouth.

"I'm not afraid, *bella*."

Her heart skipped at the endearment even though he pronounced it with such lethal warning. "Then come with me," she dared.

He snorted at her audacity and reached

across to cup the side of her neck. The possessive action was enough to heat her blood afresh.

She understood then that she had placed herself in the palm of his hand. The sense of obligation Niko had held over her was nothing compared to the casual dominance Val could exert with a smoky look at her mouth or the sensual caress of his fingertip against her nape.

"You understand that you're mine now? I respect the delicate artist within you, so I will give you this gift, but you will only bring what is truly yours. Nothing of that man will enter my house."

Tears came into her eyes. She didn't understand it, but its roots might have been in shame. Her allegiance was shifting—had shifted—to Val, whether he deserved her devotion or not. The hours of entrusting him with her body had left her feeling exactly as he'd said. His. And his hatred of Niko was so palpable, she felt disloyal for the years she'd spent with him.

"Say thank you."

"Grazie," she whispered, tentative with his language.

"I like hearing Italian from your swollen lips. And you're very pretty with your limpid eyes and whisker-burned chin but come here and say it properly." He pushed his chair back and his robe parted, exposing his chest and stomach and the thickening flesh between his powerful thighs.

She went.

Val's heart iced over as the enormous villa came into view and continued to harden as the helicopter landed on the pad behind it, exactly as it had four times a year when he'd been a child.

Run up to the green chair. Whoever gets there first can have cake.

Let them fight. Boys will be boys.

Why are you making trouble? That's a good school. Be grateful for the lesson.

He kept his mirrored aviators on as they disembarked, but the blinding white walls of the villa still hurt his eyes. His first breath of island air propelled him back in time, provoking an old, sick tension in his gut that warned him he would disappoint no matter what he did or how hard he tried.

The sprawling, three-story building had been kept well, but looked smaller than he remembered. Had there always been only six steps up to the back door? Why had it always felt like a full flight to the gallows?

"Ready?" Kiara asked beside him.

He had bought her a new dress and yes, it had been a means of stamping his possession on her, but he had wanted to see her in a brighter color. The chartreuse green accentuated her dark eyes and made her skin glow.

Maybe it was all the sex. Few women matched his appetite, but after they'd exhausted each other into a deep sleep, she had turned to him early this morning, hands sliding without hesitation beneath the sheets to wake him.

"Don't gloat," she had pleaded.

His mouth had quickly been too busy for that and he was too irritated with himself for giving in and coming here to do anything of the kind now.

"Being here doesn't require plucking up courage," he said flatly. "It's more about suppressing the urge to vomit."

"That's not what I meant. Are you ready for—"

The door opened and a woman with a toddler in her arms said, "We heard the helicopter."

"Mummy!" Aurelia launched herself at Kiara. "I mitt you!"

"Oh, lovey." Kiara caught the sprite and hugged her tight, swiveling back and forth as she did. "I missed you, too."

Val wasn't ready. Seeing Aurelia on screen hadn't prepared him for the aura of sheer joy that seemed to radiate off her as she pulled back, tiny arms and legs clinging to Kiara while they exchanged a peck.

"I'll keep her with me," Kiara said to the woman Val realized was the nanny. "You can finish packing."

The young woman nodded and disappeared.

"Where did you go?" Aurelia asked, still on Kiara's hip.

"Remember I said Auntie Scarlett was having her baby? He's called Locke."

"I want to see him."

"She said she would send me a picture later. Right now I want you to meet someone else. This is—"

Her mouth hung open as they both seemed to realize that they hadn't discussed how she would introduce him to their daughter.

"Papà," Val said, feeling as though the ground shifted beneath him.

Kiara's smile took a split second to cement itself, but then she said, "We're going with Papà to his house."

Aurelia looked at him, one arm still firmly curled around her mother's neck as she decided what she thought of him.

For his part, Val was absorbing an instinctual sense of *mine*. Not ownership, but a primordial recognition he'd never experienced before. It was probably what he should have felt toward his father or mother—a sense of kinship or being alike. He had never experienced it so strongly with them, but when he looked at Aurelia, for the first time in his life, he knew she was a part of some abstract collective they both belonged to. She was *his*.

"I have to pack some things from my studio," Kiara said to Aurelia. "Would you like to show Papà your slide?"

Aurelia nodded and they went through the house to the side door. Kiara disappeared into the old guest bungalow, leaving the door open. Val took note of Aurelia's climbing gym and empty wading pool, the miniature picnic table and the cat that appeared and rubbed against his leg.

Niko hadn't provided anything like this for him and Javiero. Val's earliest memories involved kicking a ball at each other or learning to swim in the cold waves of the sea because learning in a pool was "soft." They'd had chores in the vineyard, raking and gathering twigs, and had listened to endless droning lectures on how they would inherit all of this and needed to know how to manage it from the bottom up.

Every conversation with Niko had been one way and about one topic—the future and what he expected of them. There had been no sense of them being good enough as they were. Niko hadn't even been mindful of the fact they were children. He hadn't been present in a meaningful way—

Neither was he, Val realized with a snap of his head. The climbing gym was empty. Aurelia was gone.

"Aurelia. No!"

The barreling shout was so loud and imperious, it arrested Kiara's heart. She dropped what she was doing and ran out to see Val running toward the pool.

The gate was open and Aurelia stood there paralyzed. When she saw Kiara, she let out a wail and lifted her arms, running toward her and tripping onto the grass as she came off the paving stones.

Kiara hurried forward and picked up her screaming toddler while Aurelia clung to her with all her wee might.

"You're fine. Settle down," Kiara murmured, rubbing her back. "You know you're not allowed in the pool without a grown-up." Kiara's own heart was pounding. As far as she'd known, Aurelia still couldn't reach the latch. She'd either grown in the past two days or the pool boy had been sloppy about closing it properly.

"I took my eyes off her for *one second*," Val muttered as he came up to them, emanating umbrage.

Kiara tried to calm Aurelia, but it took effort to keep her agitation from her voice. "Listen, baby. Papà thought you were going to get hurt. He didn't mean to scare you." She sent him a pointed glance.

"That went both ways," he retorted sharply.

"Fair enough, but maybe dial back the volume to an age-appropriate two. You scared *me*, yelling like that."

His mouth flattened as he looked at Aurelia, who was keeping her face firmly turned from his, still bawling her heart out, tiny body quivering. Remorse creased his expression along with lingering concern. "My heart completely stopped."

"Welcome to being a parent."

He jolted at that and watched her continue

rubbing Aurelia's back as she wound down to sniffles.

"We're working on our apology skills," Kiara told Val and tucked her chin to address her daughter. "Would you like to tell Papà you're sorry for giving him a fright?"

"No, Mummy." She began to sob again, this time more pitifully.

"Aurelia, I'm sorry," Val said quietly and sincerely. His hand came up as though he wanted to touch her, but he hesitated at the last second and let it drop back to his side. "I shouldn't have yelled. I was afraid you were going to fall in the water. I may yell again if I'm afraid for you, but I'm not angry. I promise I will never, *ever* hurt you. Please don't be afraid of me."

Kiara was pretty sure Val had never apologized to anyone. Ever. She melted from the inside out, limbs going so weak she could barely hold on to her daughter.

"Do you have something you want to say to Papà?" She prodded Aurelia in a husky voice.

"I'm torry," Aurelia said, lifting her heartbroken, tear-tracked face.

As naturally as if she'd been doing it from the moment she had arrived on this earth, she tipped out of Kiara's arms and went to her father for a make-up cuddle.

He caught her with an audible inhale of surprise and then released a shaken exhale.

Kiara's defenses crumbled to nothing then, as she watched the impact of Aurelia's freely offered love hit Val like a meteorite. The glimmer of something flashed and shattered in his eyes before he closed them, yet he failed to hide his emotions as he cradled her tiny form against his chest. He hung his head over her, and his brow pulled with torment, as though he had indeed rescued Aurelia from the bottom of the pool.

Or she had rescued him.

Kiara pressed a hand to her chest, trying to keep her heart from breaking through her rib cage, while Aurelia let her head settle on Val's shoulder and stuck two fingers in her mouth. Tears still stood on her cheeks as she blinked at her mother, but her trust in her father had been secured.

* * *

Eight hours later Val removed Kiara's charcoal sketch from where it hung between the pair of tall, double doors that led onto the master suite's balcony. He didn't glance out at his nonstop view of Lake Como or down to where the architect and his team were discussing retaining walls and rooflines.

His palms briefly felt the dig of the sleek chrome edges as his hands tightened on the frame, but he didn't allow himself to get lost in reminiscence. He moved it to a high shelf in his walk-in closet and brushed his hands together, angry with himself for feeling compelled to hide that he'd not only kept her sketch, he'd also had it matted, framed and mounted in his bedroom.

It seemed a greater weakness to let Kiara see it, though. And he was already reeling under the punch that had been Aurelia. He'd overreacted on the island, he knew that, but in the moment of realizing she'd slipped away into the pool area, he'd been utterly terrified. Convinced he wouldn't reach her before she drowned.

She might have been gone before he'd felt the weight of her head on his shoulder. Before he'd allowed her to crawl on him like a kitten as they traveled, showing him her handful of books and favorite toys. She would have been gone before she'd clung to his finger as she jumped the stepping stones down to the lower terrace so Kiara could approve the site for her new studio. Gone before he'd known that she was bright and curious and stubborn and had a giggle that filled his heart with joy.

He had known she could become a vulnerability for him, but he hadn't *known*.

She wasn't an exposed flank; she was an offered throat. He couldn't bear it. He most especially resented that Kiara knew what was happening to him. A dewy smile appeared on her face every time Aurelia said *Papà* in her high, musical voice.

"Oh…um—" Kiara walked in and came up short as she saw him hovering in the middle of the room. "I was looking for my things. The maid said this was my room."

A mad craving leaped in his blood at the sight of her. It was another weakness, born in a single night of losing himself with her, and it further undermined his sense of self and autonomy.

"This is our room. Our bed," he acknowledged with a nod toward the wide mattress, liking the flush of awareness that stained her cheeks. He needed the surge of power that filled him as he saw he could turn her on with a careless few words the same way she could light his fires just by appearing in front of him.

"It's not a his and hers...?" She warily looked for a connecting door in the expansive room, but there was only the door into the bathroom and the one into the closet. Presently, the room had a cozy sitting area and a desk, but he expected there would be some changes to balance the masculine decor with some feminine touches.

"I bought this villa after the divorce and didn't expect to marry again," he explained.

Her little frown of consternation eased slightly. Perhaps she'd been bothered by the idea of sleeping in his ex-wife's bed.

"Well, I just came to get changed." She

plucked at the shoulder of her dress where Aurelia looked to have cried herself to sleep.

He waved at the closet.

Kiara hesitated, then closed the bedroom door and stayed near it.

"I'm sorry about the meltdown." She released an exasperated breath that lifted a corkscrew of hair out of her eyes. "Tantrums are fairly normal at her age, but she doesn't usually go nuclear like that. I think it was a combination of missing me last night and all the new faces today." Aurelia had screamed bloody murder when Kiara had tried to hand her off to the nanny for her nap. "She'll probably be out of sorts until we find our routine here."

She eyed him warily, perhaps expecting an indictment on her inability to discipline their daughter, but the kickup hadn't fazed him.

"I've seen far worse displays from my mother over far less."

Kiara gave a short laugh, but he was completely serious. She sobered.

"Well, I'm glad you don't think less of her for it. She's only little and still figuring things out." And there was that starry look again, lips curving into an emotive smile.

She wanted another glimpse of the man whose armor had been breached and he refused to give it to her, hardening against her melting look.

Her gaze lowered and her lashes fluttered with brief confusion.

"I'm a little out of sorts myself," she confessed, clutching her elbows, flashing him an upward look. "This must feel like an invasion of your space."

He shrugged it off. "As a child, I had a lot of surprises thrust upon me. I learned to adapt very quickly."

"Witness the installation of your child and her mother in your home barely twenty-four hours after learning about her."

Plus, two nannies and a *cat*.

"I prefer to act, not react," he said truthfully, even though he was reacting to her against his will as she moved cautiously into the room, trailing her fingers across the smooth polish on the desk and picking up a stray bottle of his sandalwood cologne for a sniff.

"I don't know what I expected, but your home is very beautiful." She glanced at the filmy dark blue of the curtain clasped back with a silver cuff. "Airy and full of textures and light."

"Mother likes a project. Of her many faults, taste is not one of them."

"I'll be sure to compliment her when I see her."

"You won't," he assured her. "I'm leaving her in time-out until she's learned her lesson about keeping things from me."

Kiara's expression grew somber. She set the bottle back on its shelf.

"And me? Am I to be punished for keeping Aurelia from you?"

"Our marriage is very much two birds with one stone." He discovered he wasn't joking about that, either. He resented her for doing this to him. Not so much the hiding of his child, but the giving him one. He could stand that his life was changing. He couldn't stand that *he* was changing. That wasn't Aurelia's fault, but Kiara knew what she was doing to him, provoking things in him. *Feelings.*

A brief wrinkle of hurt pinched her brow and he braced himself for the inevitable refusal to marry him.

She surprised him by asking with quiet dignity, "Do you know what I find striking about you and me? That we're both determined to be the thing we hate most about ourselves. After my mother died, I didn't matter to anyone. I tried to fit in, but I was a square peg in every cliquey circle. The subtle rejections became too much for me. I decided friends were overrated and took introversion to its furthest degree. It was lonely, but it was safe. So there's a part of me that prefers you to hate me and block me out. Then I can tell myself that trying to have a relationship with you is futile. I can refuse to marry you and retreat behind my walls. While you want me to believe that tying myself to you is a life sentence because you're such a terrible man."

"I'm not a good one," he scoffed.

"Why not?" She cocked her head. "I mean, I understand that other people told you that you weren't. And that you were angry with Niko and did whatever you thought you had to, to cut ties with him. But why is bitter misery such a comfortable place for either of us? I have to believe you have redeeming qualities, Val, otherwise, why am I here? And you have to believe I feel genuine remorse and forgive me for keeping Aurelia a secret. Otherwise, we have no hope, and a life without hope is a very dark place."

Blows and insults and disparagement he could take. Her incisive honesty, however, peeled layers off him, leaving him raw and exposed. He couldn't bear it and reached for the quickest, easiest means of turning the tables on her.

"I warned you against swimming with sea monsters."

He ambled across to her, watching her eyes widen as he did. The glimmer of misplaced faith in her gaze dimmed to apprehension. Some distant, misguided part of himself wanted to preserve that hopeful gleam as badly as he wanted to dispel it.

He cupped the side of her throat and felt her swallow.

"I will be gentle with our daughter because

she is a child, but whatever tenderness you think is inside me is imaginary. I never forgive people who wrong me." He scraped his thumb across her bottom lip to pull it free from the wary catch of her teeth. "I never trust them again."

"So you'll—what? Get revenge by making hate to me, not love?" she asked shakily, color rising in reaction to his touch.

"That would imply I have strong feelings for you." He would squelch such things before they sprouted. "No, you matter to me only insofar as it gives me incredible pleasure to watch you surrender to passion. So I'll exact that sort of compensation from you again and again, because I like it. But I will never offer you a piece of my soul."

"And if I say no to that?" Beneath his palm, her carotid artery was a rapid tattoo.

"Can you?" he chided, allowing his gaze to travel down to where her breasts were quivering as she panted in growing arousal.

He needed that. Needed to see that she was powerless against this force of lust between them because its grip on him was so inexorable, he could hardly breathe.

He brought his free hand up and rippled his knuckles across the point of her nipple where it strained against the cup of her bra and the fabric of her dress. Lightly, lightly, so the only sound was the faint brush of skin on linen. A straining silence that stretched and stretched as he moved his fingers back and forth, until she made a small noise and clasped his wrist, stopping his teasing caress.

"That's—" A small sob escaped her.

"Too much?" he asked, dropping his hand to weigh heavily on her hip. "Or not enough?"

She clenched her eyes shut in sensual struggle.

"Come here, little mermaid," he coaxed mockingly. "Let the monster take a bite."

With a choke of capitulation, she moved forward to press against him.

He did bite her. He gently grazed his smiling teeth against the side of her neck until she trembled and arched and sighed. Then he showed her *exactly* how much penance he could wring out of her.

* * *

As retribution went, his was all the more powerful for its thrilling, torturous highs and her soaring abandonment of self. Val kissed her until she could barely stand, then he made her stand there before him anyway, skirt bunched around her waist, wrists pinned in one of his strong hands behind her back while he lowered her panties only enough to taste her until she whimpered.

Then he knelt her on the sofa cushions and stood behind her, thrusting lazily into her while she grasped at the slippery, striped silk. He brought her to such a peak, she didn't care if people heard her pleasured cries across the lake.

He took her to the bed, stripped her and licked every inch of her, until she was nothing but one throbbing nerve ending, then he entered her again, made her come again, strong arms tucked behind her knees. Still, he wasn't finished. He tumbled her across the bed until he was sitting on the edge and she was in his lap.

Oh, he pretended to love her then. He

soothed and caressed and teased and incited until she was writhing. And all the while, the stiff thickness of him filled her. Each twist and arch of her body was stifled by strong arms as he fought his own release while provoking her to the very limits of her endurance of pleasure.

Only when she was running mindless fingers through his hair moaning, "Please, Val, please," through swollen lips that clung to his did he shift her onto her back again and thrust steadily into her, keeping her on that acute point of unbearable arousal.

"Soon, *bella*," he crooned, body shaking with exertion and the strain of maintaining his control. "When I say. Not before."

"I can't, I can't," she moaned, so close she was dying. She wanted so badly to let climax overtake her, but she fought it. For him. Because he wished it.

"Now," he growled with a plunge of his hips.

The world went supernova. Her vision turned white, her scream silent, her only thought *yes* as orgasm exploded through her.

Shock wave after shock wave of intense pleasure was made all the more exquisite for the pulsing heat within her and the ragged call of her name in Val's triumphant voice.

Kiara slipped out of bed and into the shower while Val was dozing, half expecting him to join her. She wanted him to, even though he had pretty much destroyed her.

He left her to shower alone, however, and she heard his voice when she was drying off. She used the adjoining door from the bathroom into the closet and discovered clothing in her size, but none of it was familiar. Still wearing the black robe that smelled of him, she crept out to find him on the balcony sharing cheese and fruit with Aurelia, teaching her the Italian names for grape and orange and peach.

"See? I told you she would join us," he said as Kiara appeared.

"Hello, lovey," she greeted her daughter warmly, then held up the clothes in her hand and said to Val, "These aren't mine."

"They are," he confirmed.

Kiara looked at the sky blue top and the indigo skirt that were super cute, but a bolder statement than she usually made. "Where are the clothes I brought?"

"I told you how I felt about his things coming into my house." He avoided using Niko's name, glancing at Aurelia as though sensitive to how she might react if he mentioned the old man. "I won't ask Mousy here to give up her attachments. She'll grow out of most of them quickly enough, but *you* will wear what *I* provide."

If their daughter's tiny, listening ears and wide, curious eyes hadn't been trained on her, Kiara might have reacted more reflexively—and heatedly—but Aurelia's presence forced her to take a breath and mentally count to ten.

She pinned a smile on her face and used a light tone but made sarcastic use of his own words. "I wanted to give you the gift of abiding by your wishes."

He narrowed his eyes.

"That's why I only brought clothes I'd bought with my own money," she continued with false cheer. "I have a little income from a handful of prints and other early works. It's not extravagant, but neither are my tastes. Which means I don't have to rely on anyone's support. Not even yours."

"But I want you to rely on me," he said, adopting a similar tone of friendly conversation to hide the fact they were engaged in an epic power struggle.

"I know what you want."

To consume her.

That had been obvious in the way he'd made love to her. She could withstand that in bed, barely, but she wouldn't let him take every shred of independence she possessed. It had been too hard won.

"I am a fashion mogul, Kiara," he said as though explaining it to a child. "That means I am under constant scrutiny for the way I look. My wife must be as much a brand ambassador as I am." He wore a plain white T-shirt over a pair of wrinkled, linen pants, casually elegant in a way she never could be.

Her stomach tightened.

"You do realize the industry will lose its collective mind if we marry? I said *if*!" she added quickly when a slow smile began to form on his lips. "I am the opposite of iconic. You couldn't have picked a worse person if your reputation is important to you."

"I think I've made it abundantly clear that I never do as I'm told. If I want my wife to have curves, then curves she shall have. The fashion world will adjust accordingly."

Dear God, if she could have a tenth of his confidence. She looked at the clothes she held.

"Klaus is my lead designer. A genius. I had him drop everything and I want to see how he did with the little direction I gave him. He's sending a team to measure you properly, by the way."

"And I promise to be ever so polite when I explain things like this aren't *me*."

"How do you know if you haven't even tried them on? I'm surprised at you, Kiara. How would you feel if people dismissed your paintings without even looking at them?" Humor made his silver eyes gleam like chrome. He had her with that one and knew it.

She pressed her lips together, annoyed in

the extreme as she flung around and went back to the closet, determined to hate this outfit.

Curse him and his designer. The cut somehow balanced her figure, so she looked taller and more evenly proportioned. There was something crisp and eye-catching in the color palette, too. Feminine without being frilly. Confident in her curves, authoritative, yet sensual.

There would be no fading into the wallpaper in clothes like this, though. She wasn't sure how she felt about that.

She returned to the balcony and Aurelia gasped. "Oh, Mummy, you're pretty!"

"Thank you, baby," she murmured, but Val's was the judgment she waited with held breath to hear.

She was doing it again, she realized as his critical eye traveled over her. She was trying to fit in, be something she wasn't, longing to earn acceptance that wouldn't come.

She hated herself then for being so needy. Still an orphan at her deepest level, yearning for a place. For love.

"I'll have Klaus remove this button." Val fingered the slit in the skirt, not even touching her, but setting her alight all the same. "It distracts from an otherwise perfect vision. Do you like it?"

His gaze came up to hers, absent of mockery, only lit with such admiration she could have fallen into his gaze like dropping through a looking glass into another world.

She tried for blasé, saying, "I wouldn't paint in it," but she did like it. Nothing felt constraining and the textures were nice. She liked that it made her feel pretty. She liked that he liked it.

Somehow, she would have to pull herself back from the brink of this chasm. Otherwise, she might allow him to take her over completely, the way he clearly intended to.

But she still obeyed his crooked finger and bent to touch her mouth to his, saying a husky *"Grazie..."* against his lips.

His taste swept through her, as irresistible as the man himself.

CHAPTER SIX

KIARA HAD KNOWN this period after Niko passed would be disruptive and she might not have as much time in her studio as she normally liked. But she hadn't counted on trying to turn a guest cottage into a makeshift studio between meetings with architects and clothing designers, decorators, and stoic lawyers who were drawing up a *marriage* contract.

She kept telling Val she wasn't ready to commit while he kept saying, "I'll be ready when you are."

Then he inevitably made love to her, showing her exactly what she would gain by becoming his wife.

She was desperately trying to retain her autonomy, trying to envision the place she would have in this world of his, but it was hard.

Her studio was usually the space that restored her. It was her sanctuary and the place where she meditated on her problems and made herself whole. The new one would take time to build, however, and Val insisted she go ahead with meetings about layout and materials and breaking ground even though she hadn't agreed to marry him.

What if she didn't? she kept wondering.

Wasted money didn't seem to faze him. He was having Klaus design her a wedding gown, too.

Perhaps Val thought if she was invested enough in her new studio, she would be unable to resist marrying him. What he didn't realize was that all of these meetings were getting between her and a return to painting. The fact she wasn't painting was putting her on edge in a way she hadn't experienced in years, not since right after Aurelia had been born and she'd been overwhelmed by her new responsibilities.

At least today Val had gone into Milan on errands. She had a feeling he was finalizing wedding arrangements, but she gratefully seized the opportunity to properly organize the bungalow into a space she could use. Then she was going to use it. She would spend a few hours with brushes and a canvas on her easel and finally decide whether to stay here with him or go back to the villa.

Oh, part of her longed to go back to the island where life was simple!

But she couldn't.

The way Aurelia was bonding with her father was everything Kiara had ever wanted for her. And Val was so patient with her, so gentle. He claimed to have no tenderness in him, but his hard features softened every time he saw her. He was turning into an amazing parent, learning the fine art of misdirection to avoid an outburst and watching their tot like a hawk while giving her space to roam and explore.

All of that was turning Kiara's heart inside out. She could see there was a good man inside him, but he only offered glimpses of him, refusing to let him fully reveal himself. She wanted to hate him for that guard of his, but she was too enthralled by the side of him he did let her see—the virile, generous lover. Being locked with him in sensual ecstasy gave her the sense of closeness and unity she'd longed for all her life. As though she'd found her match. The place she belonged.

But it was demoralizing to be so defenseless when he was always in control of everything from their lovemaking to the cadence of their days. He never seemed as rent from the world as she was by their physical encounters. He withdrew afterward without words of affection or fondness. He might compliment her and hold chairs and make endless requests of the staff on her behalf, but she was certain he would have done that for any woman who shared his bed.

Given the way he was withholding his heart, she knew she couldn't offer hers. It would only be trampled and destroyed, but it was a struggle every hour of every day. One she didn't know if she could withstand for a lifetime.

"Scusami..." A timid maid knocked on the open sliding door.

Kiara bit back a scream. She had expressly

asked that she not be disturbed and realized that she would have to train the staff that when she said that, she meant it.

"*Signora* Casale has arrived to see you," the maid said.

Kiara's heart lurched. At least Aurelia was firmly ensconced upstairs. They'd had a lively morning in the pool, and she was pooped out, watching a show and having a snack with the nanny.

Kiara hadn't bothered with a shower, too anxious to get to work. She had ruthlessly sleeked her hair back into a ponytail, but the ends ballooned out in a cloud of frizz behind her head. She wore painting clothes of jeans chopped at the knee and a loose T-shirt.

She had an urge to run up and put on a decent day dress but decided against it. She doubted it was coincidence that Evelina had shown up the moment Val was out of the house. Kiara refused to give Evelina the impression she was intimidated—even though she absolutely was.

"What a lovely surprise," she lied as she entered the lounge to find Evelina hovering with a sour look on her face. "Shall we have tea on the terrace?"

Her potential mother-in-law wore six-inch heels, a pencil skirt and an air of malicious intent. She towered over Kiara as they walked outside.

"The house is beautiful. Your influence, Val tells me," Kiara said, trying on a compliment as they settled into an outdoor lounge around an unlit gas fire.

"Yes. I have so many excellent contacts eager to assist me at any time. Many of them are in Paris." Evelina crossed one graceful leg over the other. "I understand you have a little art show there next week."

The implication was obvious and it made Kiara's stomach turn over.

Kiara realized then how often she had ducked behind Niko or Scarlett in the past. *Tell me what to say*, she would often implore, even when she only faced a friendly business conversation with her agent. She was tempted to invoke Val's name as a shield but being used as a weapon was the reason Val was as cynical as he was. Besides, much as she wanted to believe he would have her back, she didn't know that for sure.

"I do. Shall I ask my agent to send you an invite?" She played dumb, as though she wasn't clear that she was being threatened in the most effective way. As if her palms weren't clammy and her throat wasn't aching with a stifled scream.

"That won't be necessary. I'm so well-known in those circles, I'm welcome wherever I wish to go. Many would say my appearance can make or break the success of a given evening. I'm prepared to speak to critics about you. It would be such a *shame* if they found your work wanting. Or failed to attend at all."

Kiara's throat closed and the backs of her eyes stung with angry, helpless tears. She fought the sensation. Hysteria wasn't an option. She racked her brain, barely able to form words, her jaw was clenched so hard.

"I wouldn't want you to feel a need to interfere." She saw a maid coming with the tea service and waved her away. "I presume this is about Niko's will. Please understand I had nothing to do with how he structured it."

"I'm not a stupid woman. I've been on my own since I was fifteen. I understand that a woman has to look out for herself and this—" she twirled a finger in the air "—was a very nice try. I'm impressed. But I have spoken to my lawyer and he agrees that Val is entitled to Niko's fortune. If you would like to relinquish all claim to it, I will see my way clear to ensuring your little show is well received."

Kiara was having trouble keeping down what little she'd eaten this morning. She knew for a fact that Evelina had a very shaky leg to stand on in making any claims against Niko's fortune, but the last thing she needed was to have her lifetime dream trampled by a battle royal.

"Val doesn't want Niko's money," she reminded quietly.

"Val doesn't know what he wants," Evelina threw back. "It most certainly isn't *you*. You're not marrying him."

"I haven't agreed to," Kiara said, adding tartly, "He brings a lot of baggage."

"You—" Evelina gathered herself the way a lightning strike might gather ions, preparing to crack the earth open. "I will *destroy* you."

Angry emotion was driving color into the skin beneath the powder of Evelina's makeup. Kiara could read it as clearly as she knew when Aurelia was building toward a tantrum.

Aurelia lost her self-control when she had no control. When Mummy said no to something she wanted.

Kiara's mind was racing through all of her options, catching on the fact that she wasn't without resources or options. She actually had something Evelina wanted that she could give up. It would cost her, but...

"I may have a solution." Kiara held up a shaking hand. "Val doesn't want me to accept the allowance I've been granted from Niko's estate. He wants to support us himself. I had a mind to put that money into real estate as an investment for Aurelia. I could be persuaded to let you choose that property and occupy the house at no cost to you. It's quite a generous amount." She told her how much.

Evelina's eyes were still flashing with acrimony, but her mouth trembled as she pinned it closed, trying to calculate how to play this.

"That's *if* I marry him. I haven't agreed," Kiara said quickly. "I can leave here and live on that myself. You and I can argue over Niko's money until the cows come home. It will be expensive and, frankly, I would think you must be tired of that fight by now."

"You underestimate me," Evelina assured her.

"Well, make up your mind however it suits you, but my offer stands. Of course, if I marry Val and our marriage falls apart—" Kiara licked her dry lips "—I will be forced to evict you so I could live there with Aurelia."

"You're buying my support of your marriage," Evelina stated bluntly. "Bribing me to keep my nose out of it."

"I see it as a smart investment in my daughter's future." She was shaking inside, skin running hot and cold.

"You *have* learned well at Niko's knee. Are you going to tell Val about this arrangement?"

"Yes." She couldn't imagine keeping something like this from him. "If you're worried he'll cut off the allowance he gives you, I'll do my best to persuade him to continue it."

Evelina didn't know whether to trust her; Kiara could see it. She wanted to sigh with futility. These people were *so* broken. Instead, she smiled as gently as she would at Aurelia when she was at her most truculent.

"You are my daughter's only grandparent. She wouldn't exist if you and Niko hadn't made Val. I think it's right and fair that you live comfortably. Perhaps, when the time is right, you'll introduce Aurelia to the best boutiques in Paris, since that is definitely not my forte. What do you say? Do we have a deal?"

Val was waiting to announce the existence of his daughter until he and Kiara were married—and they would marry. Aurelia's future and well-being were too important to risk. Any misgivings Kiara had could be worked out after the fact.

Her hesitation was bothering him, though. Especially because it was accompanied by a withdrawal that shouldn't have gotten under his skin but did.

At night she was wholly his, completely abandoned to the pleasure they gave each other. Then she would spend the day pulling back in little ways. If she happened to be laughing or playing with Aurelia, her mood would dampen when he entered the room. Over a meal, she would grow animated as she spoke, then cool unexpectedly, as though regretting she had allowed herself to warm to him. She was forever switching the focus of a conversation from herself to their daughter, avoiding his attempts to learn more about her.

Outright challenge he could handle, but she went along with most of his dictates unless they concerned Aurelia. Then she would put forth an argument with calm logic. He would only realize she'd been on the defensive when her shoulders fell after winning him over to her way of thinking.

He didn't like a quiet enemy that kept him guessing.

He didn't want to think of her as an enemy at all. He was too enthralled with her.

He dragged her physically close every chance he got. Stripped her naked so there were no barriers between them, insatiable for her and their particular brand of madness. *Connection.* This thing between them was reaching the point of addiction, and he'd finally left her sleeping this morning just to prove he could.

He drove to Milan, determined to be his old self and put in a long day—despite the fact he would ensure the first of the banns were posted. After that, news of his engagement would begin making headlines across the usual gossip sites, drawing out the paparazzi.

It was a dirty move, putting that kind of pressure on her. It was exactly the sort of ruthless tactic he was known for, so he wasn't sure why it ruffled his conscience. This was who he *was.*

He was a cutthroat corporate raider completely lacking in empathy or compassion. That was why he was browsing for toys himself, wandering store aisles, picking up dolls that annoyed him because they were so sexualized. He gathered crafts instead, and puzzles, and building blocks, and a child-safe baby drill with plastic pieces that would hurt like hell to step on, but gender expectations could go to hell. Aurelia could be whoever she wanted to be.

He never gave gifts, not thoughtful ones, only corporate nonsense. As for receiving them, aside from the warehouses of free samples that arrived daily, with pleas for him to feature them in one of his many magazines, he had only received one real gift in his lifetime—and he'd basically stolen it. Kiara's sketch.

The blank space on his bedroom wall was only obvious to him, but it made him uneasy each time he looked for the sketch and didn't see it. It was similar to looking for the laughing woman who'd drawn it and finding only the subdued, unreadable expression on Kiara's beautiful face.

Maybe he was being too hard on her, he thought as he drove home—early, hoping to catch her while Aurelia was down for her afternoon nap. Maybe Kiara was right. Maybe he did have to forgive her for colluding with his father. Maybe then she wouldn't be so apprehensive about marrying him.

Then he heard that she'd entertained a visitor while he'd been out. The identity of that visitor was like blood in the water to a shark.

Kiara was still shaken, still questioning whether she'd made the right choice.

She had. For Aurelia. She knew that much. But this situation was testing her more severely than anything else in her life. Her own needs were being pitted against her daughter's, and Kiara still wasn't sure whether she was winning, losing or falling for a con.

Because she was still here in Italy, not on a plane back to Greece and, after that conversation with Evelina, she had pretty much thrown away her chance to make an escape.

She didn't even *like* confrontation, let alone playing hardball with a pro. Her hands were still shaking as she finally set up her easel.

These trembles were promising a very poor result when she got a brush in her hand, but she was fixated now. If she could just paint something—not even with serious intent, more like journaling—she would find her equilibrium and be okay. She would be able to face this new life she had accidentally embarked upon.

"You met with my mother today?"

The growl of Val's voice was so unexpected and lethal, she almost knocked over her easel.

"You're home," she said dumbly, whirling to the open door.

"Surprised?" He strode in, flicking the sliding door closed behind him with a thud that held such aggression she frowned. "Oh, don't even *think* of locking *me* out of your studio."

Her heart was skinned and overworked from all the conflicts and hard conversations and massive changes she'd suffered since the doctor had pronounced Niko "gone." Now it flip-flopped and shrank and quavered at the way he loomed over her.

This was the man she had backed herself into marrying?

"I didn't know what to do except offer her tea," she said stiffly, moving to find a prepared canvas.

"Tea," he scoffed.

"Was I supposed to slam the door in her face?"

"Yes."

"I wish I had," she blurted, managing to set the canvas and pry her tense fingers off it without throwing it across the room. "It wasn't exactly a 'welcome to the family' visit." More like a viper popping out of a harmless-looking hatbox.

"Did she see Aurelia?" His tone crackled with danger.

"No." Kiara crossed her arms defensively, but shot her shoulders back, willing to die on the hill of making that decision, not that Evelina had *asked* to meet her granddaughter.

A fraction of Val's enmity receded, but he still glowered with accusation. "What did you two cook up, then? Because she's not here. That means she got what she wanted. Don't even try to tell me you're leaving," he warned.

Kiara's stomach was still full of gravel over the entire thing, but now her blood hit full boil at the way he was treating her like she was some sort of criminal. Like she'd orchestrated the meeting. She'd been the victim. Ambushed!

"She *wanted* to destroy my show." Her voice cracked as she relived hearing that threat. Her whole body was plunged back into the fight or flight that had gripped her while she had talked herself out of a hostage situation.

"You know I will undo any damage she attempts," Val said on a growl.

"No, I don't know that!" she cried on a choke of humorless laughter. "Every time I turn around, you're looking for a new way to punish me for relying on your father. Losing my show would be the ultimate revenge and probably make you very happy. So no, Val. I fixed it myself. Thanks anyway."

His head went back, and he narrowed his eyes. "How?"

"I bought her off with Niko's money, of course! I told her you didn't want me to touch my living allowance, but I thought it should be invested for Aurelia's future. I said that if she found a suitable property that would appreciate over time, I would direct those funds into purchasing a home for her and she could have the use of it for her lifetime."

His eyebrows climbed into his hairline.

"Then I told her that if our marriage broke down for any reason, like an interfering mother-in-law, I'd have to evict her so Aurelia and I could use it, so she had better think long and hard in the future about which battles are important to her." Her throat was still scorched by all the adrenaline that had coursed through her. It was still there, searing her limbs and making her heart run so fast she was exhausted.

Val swore. Snorted and spoke with what sounded like reluctant admiration. "You're a quick study. Well-done."

She had been fighting for her very existence, but okay. Sure. *Scoff away.*

She turned to find her smock.

Val was still bristling that his mother had had the gall to show up uninvited and that Kiara had let her in. Even more infuriating was the fact she had caught Kiara alone. That told him he had a mole in his home. Heads would roll over that, but he wasn't finished with Kiara.

Losing my show would be the ultimate revenge.

He preferred to be angry with her. It was easier to hold her at a distance when he had that resentment between them, but surely she knew he would shield her against real harm of any kind? If she didn't believe that, it made her still being here a profound statement, given the vile threat his mother had used to try running her off.

That surprising show of loyalty sawed holes in his defenses against her.

"Come here," he coaxed, wanting the feel of her to erase the gnawing ache in his chest.

"I thought I'd finally get some painting in." The enticing fit of her cutoff jeans over her round bottom and shapely thighs disappeared as she shrugged into what looked like an old lab coat bedecked in years of paint smears. She didn't look at him as she began to button it.

He crossed to still her hands.

"Come on, *bella*. Let's kiss and make up.

I'll make it worth your while," he coaxed, stroking his thumbs across the backs of her hands, smiling at the way they trembled.

"Are we fighting? I thought this was our normal, where you blame me for your parents' actions and I put your daughter's needs ahead of my own." She pulled her hands from his and opened the buttons she'd closed, voice quavering as she continued. "But if you want to have sex, by all means, let's have sex. Why did I even engage in hand-to-hand combat with your mother if not to keep having sex with you?"

An anvil hit the pit of his gut. "If you don't want to have sex—"

"I always want to have sex!" she cried, throwing down her coat. "But I *need* to paint, Val. I haven't held a brush since before Niko died and it's killing me!"

"You're in here every day." Usually after Aurelia had gone to bed, before they sat down for their own dinner. "What have you been doing?" He glanced around at the cleared space where furniture had been removed, the stacks of blank canvases against the wall and the shelf where tins and trays of brushes and other supplies were arranged.

"Everything but painting," she said in a voice that was still strident. Her arms flailed helplessly. "I've been unpacking and organizing. Scrambling out sketches of how my paintings should be displayed at the show, answering emails about it. Do you know I had to write descriptions for each one? And that I have *revisions*? My artist's statement wasn't good enough, so I have to rewrite *that*. I paint because I don't know *how* to express myself in words."

She was shaking, eyes brimming with fresh tears.

"Kiara," he said soothingly.

"Don't you dare tell me to calm down," she warned with a raised finger. "This is not a tantrum. This is a breakdown." Her mouth was wobbling, and she used the inside of her wrist to wipe the tears off her cheeks. "I used to paint when Aurelia slept, but now it's all you. Sex and *this*." She circled her palm through the air. "The blame. The contempt for the choices I've made. The demand that

I completely change my life while the one thing *I* want gets further away."

She clutched her chest as she sucked in a breath that shuddered. Her wild gaze swung around the room as though she didn't know where she was.

"If this is what you want, if your punishment is to push me to the point of breaking, you're there, Val. I am going to snap in half if I can't paint. Then I won't be me anymore. I'll be like you and your mother. A damaged human being incapable of love. Sorry, Aurelia, but Mummy is one more casualty of Niko's war."

Her last words struck like a sledgehammer, reverberating through him.

He did want to tell her to calm down. He wanted to take her by the arms and remind her he was building her a studio, wasn't he? Of course he wanted her to paint. He wasn't *a damaged human being*. He was matured by experience to an enlightened one.

"Why are you still dressed?" she added caustically, lashes damp. "Work your magic.

Make me forget I ever wanted this," she choked.

He consciously fought the jerky reflex trying to lift his arms to reach for her. Everything in him wanted to coil his arms around her and hold her tight until her shaking stopped. To kiss away those tears that tracked down her face. Until this grim darkness that had taken hold of her eased back into the warm light he hadn't appreciated until it had been eclipsed.

He wanted to blame his mother for this. A visit with her left anyone full of poison and spewing venom, but this wasn't all Evelina. This was him trying so hard to control what was happening between them, he was crushing the spirit out of Kiara.

He knew what he had to do, and it went against everything in him. He *never* walked away from a fight.

But if he didn't leave her now, he would make love to her until she was too weak to lift a finger.

And she wouldn't forgive him for it. He knew that in his soul. Something would be damaged between them that would never be repaired.

"I'll eat with Aurelia and put her to bed this evening. Stay in here as long as you like."

Walking out and closing the door on her stunned expression was the hardest thing he'd done in a long, long while. The angry bastard in him balked, told him to get back in there and assert his will.

But something else flickered inside him, an ember of heat he couldn't name, it was so old and forgotten. Hope? Caring? It retained some heat, whatever it was. Just enough to ease the frigid cold that encased his heart.

It was after midnight when Kiara slid into bed.

She was exhausted, but alert. Buzzing with excitement. *Revived.*

She had steeped herself in the scent of her linen canvas and the wood stretchers and the nutty smell of the oil paints. She had danced her brush into color, conducted a symphony, tapped it into solvent, then swirled and done it again. She had dazzled herself with colors and lost herself in a world where hurtful people couldn't touch her. Where her emotions ran free, rather than trying to fit into ever-shrinking boxes.

She couldn't recall when she'd last painted like that, in a flurry from blank canvas to completion. Not that the finished product was anything worth showing off, but it would forever be a favorite for its claiming of this new world and thus the reclaiming of herself.

And now she was overwhelmed with gratitude toward Val for giving her that. Each time she had come up for air and thought of Aurelia, she had remembered she was with her father. Leaving her in his care was different than leaving her to the nannies. Giving Val and Aurelia time to bond was as important as the time she spent alone with their daughter.

He had even sent over a tray of finger foods that she'd picked at while she painted.

Was he awake? She slithered closer, heart off center as she remembered her eruption of fury. He could have dismissed her or tried to make her talk out her frustrations and hurts and anxiety, but he hadn't. He'd let her work through it in her own way. In the way that made sense to her.

She found warm naked skin. His abdomen tightened as she smoothed her hand across the firm muscles and the light trail of hair. His breath hissed.

He didn't say anything, though, and neither did she. She only stretched herself alongside him with a sigh of homecoming. She was as naked as he was, her nightgown never lasting long, but tonight she was the instigator. She brushed her mouth across his once as she pressed over him, then skated her parted lips down his throat and across his shoulders.

His strong hands clasped her and pulled her fully onto him. His legs parted for hers and she lifted slightly to allow his thickening flesh room to grow against her stomach. She used her whole body to caress him, loving the feel of his strength, the scent on his skin, the possessive, inciting roam of his hands over her back and butt and the sides of her breasts.

Desire ran like honey in her and she poured it over him. Poured herself over him along with all the uplifting, invigorating energy she had soaked up while creating.

Down, down she went, dislodging the sheet as she found the steely shape that thrilled her. Here was the essence of him, salty and musky and fierce. She anointed and played her tongue across his erotic shape, took him into her mouth and pulled, bobbing her head in the rhythm she knew he liked.

He snarled and spread his legs, tangled his fingers in her hair, pulling her away when he was about to lose control. Dragging her up, he kissed her and rolled her beneath his weight, thrust his straining flesh into her.

They groaned and gasped and hissed and writhed. It was so good she thought she might die, but it was different. He was with her in this place where reality ceased to exist. This was how it had been that night in Venice— two lost souls finding one another in the dark and celebrating the end to solitude.

She closed her ankles behind his back, and his fingers bit so hard into her bottom, he would leave bruises on her cheeks. She didn't care. She only needed him deeper. Within her. Part of her, the way she was becoming a part of him.

Culmination hit them at the same time, anguish and ecstasy, loss and discovery. An ending, but also a beginning.

Val held her all night, a fact Kiara only became aware of when he carefully extricated from her as morning light sliced through the blinds.

She blinked in confusion as he walked out of the closet seconds after he'd walked in, still naked, but with something in his hands. It was the size of a sofa cushion, but flat and shiny. He walked across to hang it on the wall, his movements sure in the half light.

She rolled over to watch, puzzled. There was no need for a hook to be screwed into the wall. He was replacing something.

She came up on an elbow, then sat up and blinked harder. She pinched her arm to ensure she wasn't dreaming.

"Don't say a word," he said quietly, touching a corner to straighten it. "Not one word."

She had to bite her lips because how? *Why?*

She stared at it like an old friend, one that filled her with a rush of nostalgic joy. She was staring so hard at it, lost in the memory of that night, she didn't realize Val had moved until he was sitting beside her on the bed, showing her a velvet box.

"I was supposed to do this over dinner last night."

Oh, God.

She started to shrink into her shoulders, but he made a dismissive noise.

"That's not a scold. I've worked with enough creatives to appreciate their temperament and know their value. I want to preserve the artist in you, Kiara," he said sincerely. "Your ability to make beauty out of nothing, to find it where none exists, is a gift." He smoothed his hand over what had to be wild hair and cupped her cheek, caressing her skin briefly with his thumb. "And after last night, I see there are advantages to giving you time to find yourself."

The dry remark was rife with self-deprecation, but teasing, too, reminding her how greedy and assertive she'd been when she'd come to bed.

She sat there boiling in self-consciousness while he leaned forward and stole a lingering kiss that relit barely banked flames between them.

Before they let passion take over, however, he drew back and opened the velvet box.

"Oh, my God."

"Val is fine," he corrected with such obscene arrogance, she would have laughed, but she was too spellbound by the three rings.

The engagement ring was a huge princess-cut diamond that picked up the narrow rays of golden sunlight. The platinum band was set with smaller diamonds interspersed with—

"Onyx?" she guessed.

"Black diamonds. Hard and dark as my heart."

He had certainly done his best to convince her of that, but he had also revealed that particular organ had flecks of gold.

She plucked out the bigger band and let it swallow her finger. "You'll wear this?"

"If you'll marry me, yes. Will you, Kiara?"

She went into a kind of free fall.

Maybe he even knew what he was doing, this wicked, crafty man. He had been trying to convince her she didn't have a choice, that she had to marry him for Aurelia's sake. She had believed it, too. But she did have a choice. And she had a suspicion it was as important to him that she *choose* him as it was for her to make this decision of her own free will.

She considered that they had a child together and an intimate relationship that showed no signs of wearing off. He respected her art and *he had kept her sketch*. He had had the charcoal fixed and framed with all the care given to the work of an Old World master.

Most important, she realized with a sharp pang in her chest as if her heart ached with yearning, she was falling for him. He might yet disappoint her. In fact, she was sure he would break her heart, probably more than once.

But that foolish heart of hers longed to go to him anyway, regardless of what her head told it.

"I will," she said huskily.

Triumph flashed in his gaze before his mouth came down on hers. She thought she heard the little box hit the floor beside the bed. The larger ring definitely fell off her finger into the sheets, but he was pressing her into the mattress and she was melting in welcome beneath him.

A faint ding pulled his head up.

She twisted a look to the night table where she left her phone each night.

"Aurelia is probably asking for you," he said.

"How was she last night?" She left her hands twined around his neck, caressing the hint of stubble she found in the hollow at the base of his skull.

"If I say fine will you dismiss the bribery charges?" He looked to his own night table. "That reminds me, I have to find a zoo with elephants. We have a date today."

To say Val softened in the ensuing days would be an overstatement, but the thorns in his personality weren't quite as pointed and sharp, at least where Kiara was concerned. He did ruthlessly fire the chef who had tipped off his mother that Kiara was alone that day. The rest of the staff was still walking on eggshells a week later.

But someone named Consuela had appeared when they returned from the zoo. She helped Kiara rewrite her statement and descriptions. She also brought a photographer to their wedding, to witness the event and prepare their press release.

"We can organize a proper wedding for later in the year if you want one," Val said as they were waiting at the courthouse.

"Goodness, no. The fact I'm having my picture taken today is giving me anxiety." But maybe it was marrying this man.

Val wore a suit for the first time since they'd been together and dear God he ought to need a warning as a dangerous substance. Aside from his tie, which had shots of silver in it, he wore all black, tailored scrupulously to his frame. The jacket was tuxedo in style with satin lapels, but had a subtle pattern embossed into it, like a smoking jacket. It should have looked affected, but it was as carelessly stylish as he always was.

He'd *shaved* and oozed so much sex appeal, Kiara's knees were weak.

She had put her faith in Klaus, who had assured her he wouldn't be working for Val if he didn't have a better eye than his boss for texture, color, line and form.

Her dress was the height of simplicity, knee-length with drop shoulders in silk colored with the barest hint of lemon yellow. The color made her skin seem luminous and the diaphanous overskirt was generous enough to gather on her arm. It fluttered and trailed with her movements, making her feel like a princess.

When Val saw her, he didn't say anything for a long moment. She thought he might have swallowed. Then he picked up her hand and slowly twirled her, saying, "Here she is. I knew she was in there." His smooth, freshly shaved cheek had brushed hers so he didn't ruin her makeup with a kiss.

It would have been a perfect day except for one thing—Scarlett wasn't here. She had gone directly to Spain with Javiero when she'd checked out of the hospital.

Kiara was trying not to take it personally that she was hearing so little from her friend. A new baby kept a mother busy. She knew that. And she didn't want to rock boats with Val by flaunting that particular friendship under his nose. She completely understood Scarlett's reluctance to do the same with Javiero, but she missed her.

She sent a photo of Aurelia in her flower girl dress and got back a photo of a sleeping Locke, wearing a onesie imprinted to look like a tuxedo.

Scarlett had texted.

We're there in spirit, which made her smile wistfully.

In every other way, her wedding was perfect. Brief, but intimate. The vows weren't sentimental, but when she spoke them, and heard Val's steady tone repeat them, Kiara felt the promise in them. She had thought the weight of his ring on her finger would feel heavy, but it was more of a touch point. A reassuring symbol of their linked lives that would be with her even when he wasn't.

When he bent his head to kiss her, a shower of sparkling light went through her, all the way to the soles of her feet. This was a real chance, a real beginning.

She hoped.

In lieu of a honeymoon, they flew to Paris a few days early. It was the opposite of romantic, despite being one of the most beautiful cities in the world. Kiara took meetings and was a bundle of nerves the whole time, only sleeping because she was exhausted by Val's attentive lovemaking.

Now that their marriage had been announced, the paparazzi was in full force. Their determination to get a photo of Aurelia bordered on criminal, and if one more person asked her about Val and how they'd met, Kiara thought she would scream.

The media interviews were pure hell, but Consuela, the goddess, had prepared her well for the most idiotic questions.

"Will your daughter follow her father and grandmother into modeling?"

"When she's old enough, she can decide for herself," Kiara murmured by rote.

Val would have said, *Over my dead body*, and Kiara felt the same, but boring answers to stupid questions helped bring the focus back to the more important ones, or so Consuela had assured her.

"Where did you learn to paint?"

"It's been a lifelong passion. I was studying art in Venice when I met Val three years ago." Kiara had been stumbling through the streets, drawing on impulse, visiting whichever museum or gallery had a free or discounted entrance fee, but Consuela had assured her no one needed to know that.

"That sounds romantic."

"It was," Kiara confirmed. Keep it simple. Tell them how to feel about it.

After the day his mother had visited, Val had been in contact with Kiara's agent. They'd restructured her show into a much more exclusive event. Most of her interviews had been conducted before a single painting had been shown to anyone. Today, hours before the official opening, her work had finally been unveiled for critics. Photographers were confined to a single room. Her more intimate portraits of Aurelia and a pregnant Scarlett remained hidden from view.

It was still a struggle to concentrate, especially because her new husband was among the handful of people wandering with slow, hollow steps through the gallery before the throngs—please let there be throngs—arrived. Or not. Maybe it would be safer if no one came. If the critics and collectors decided they hated her work, she wanted as few people as possible to witness her humiliation.

Her stomach was nothing but snakes and butterflies as they sat in the backseat of his car, returning to the hotel to get ready for tonight.

"You're folding in on yourself again, *bella.* I don't like it," he said quietly.

She shot him a look. "I'm nervous as hell."

"Why?"

"Why?" She choked out a humorless laugh.

"What if they don't like it? All that work, all those years of *kidding* myself—"

He reached across and squeezed her hand, frowning when he felt how clammy and cold it was.

"You weren't kidding yourself. Do you want to know what I was thinking as I saw everything for the first time?"

"No," she lied in an anxious whisper, squeezing his hand so hard, her nails were probably cutting into his skin.

"I was thinking that you made the right decision. I don't like it. I will always see it as a deal with the devil, but I've pulled some cold-blooded moves in my time for results that were far less meaningful. Your work is profound. Standing in front of each painting, I felt what you felt when you were painting it. Curiosity, frustration, joy. The one of Aurelia…?" He brought her hand to his mouth and kissed her knuckles, leaving her shaking inside. "Your love for her is depthless, isn't it?"

"Do you think everyone is going to experience them like that?" she asked with mounting horror. "Because that makes me feel naked. I don't think I can bear it."

He made a noise of pity. "Come here, then. Let me show you that being naked has its advantages."

And if the car had cooled in the underground parking lot before they climbed out, and she couldn't meet the eyes of the driver smoking a discreet distance away, such was the consequence of being the wife of an incorrigible rake like Val Casale.

CHAPTER SEVEN

VAL WAS IN TROUBLE. He had known it when he had left Kiara to paint that night. He had known it when the compulsion to put her sketch back on the wall had forced him from the comfortable bed and the press of her warm body to his. He had known it when sliding his ring onto her finger had made something click inside his chest that locked them together and felt *good*.

He had known it when he had wandered the gallery earlier and was so awed and moved, he had ceased to care how she had made it happen; he'd simply been overwhelmed with pride and admiration that she'd done it.

And he knew it when a floral arrangement arrived at their penthouse suite.

He was nursing a drink, waiting for Kiara to finish dressing, when the courier arrived.

He handed Val the certificate of authenticity and left the packing box for the vase as he departed.

The hourglass vase was handblown by a Venetian artist, Val learned from the certificate. The mosaic of gold that spiraled in a ribbon from lip to base had been painstakingly applied to the scorching glass through an ancient technique mastered by few in this modern age. The fragrant flowers, arranged to resemble fireworks, had been chosen to symbolize luck and success.

Val had not ordered these flowers. He had given his wife a ridiculously expensive diamond necklace with matching earrings to celebrate her achievement.

This had better be from her agent, he decided, as a green haze fogged his vision and curdled his gut. If it came from any other man, he would start by knocking over the vase, then hunt down the interloper and do the same to him.

Was he *jealous*? Jealousy was a symptom of insecurity. He knew that because he'd had a front row seat to that emotion his entire life.

Uncomfortable with that insight, he flipped the card and ran his finger beneath the flap to unseal it, completely disregarding the fact it was addressed to Kiara. It was written in flowing calligraphy, likely by the florist, but the message was personal.

K.

Is break a leg *appropriate in this circumstance?*

I am so sorry to miss your big night. I know you'll knock 'em dead.

Enjoy every second and call me soon to tell me all about it.

I miss you!

Love
Scarlett, Javiero and Locke

The clip of a woman's heel sounded on the parquet floor.

He glanced up and felt the whoosh of a train headed straight toward him.

She wore patent leather boots that went up to her *thighs*. Her bronze coatdress was tailored satin and ended a few inches above the boots. Her hair had been pulled flat to her scalp then the tight curls arranged on the top of her head to resemble an offset beret. Her earrings dangled brightly while her necklace was a subtle glint from her turned-up collar.

She started to roll her lips together uncertainly but seemed to remember at the last second that they were outlined in metallic gold. She swept ridiculously long eyelashes down, revealing the shimmering shades on her lids.

"Is it too much?"

"It is exactly enough of too much," he assured her. "I'm not going to survive the drive to the gallery, let alone the rest of the night." He held out his hand, wanting her to come to him. Wanting her close even though he couldn't touch. "You're a vision."

She came across and ran light fingers down the lapel of his tuxedo. "I thought we were going to my art show, not spying on the Russians in a film noir."

"Well, there are things you don't know about me, aren't there?"

Her smile of amusement was a burst of sunshine in his chest.

He was in so much trouble.

"Are those for me? Val," she scolded, leaning to inhale the blossoms.

"They're not from me." He picked up the card and handed it to her. "Scarlett and company."

"Oh." Her smile turned poignant as she read.

"Have you been talking with her?" He hated the talons of threat that dug into him, forcing the question from him.

"Not much," she murmured with a small, brooding frown. "A few texts, mostly about diaper rash and other baby questions. It's an overwhelming time for her. I wish I could be there more." She set aside the card and lifted a troubled gaze to him. "I wish I understood why you and Javiero are still so completely at odds."

"He knows what he did," Val said flatly, only hearing how his dismissive words had come down like an ax when Kiara flinched.

"I didn't mean to pry," she murmured, gaze bruised.

And that, too, pulled apart things inside him.

"Kiara." He held her before him, the most bizarre impulse to tell her rising in him.

No. That part of his life had been kicked into the farthest corner of a vault, the thick door slammed and welded shut. He had spoken once about it and got nothing for his trouble. He had sworn he would never speak of it again.

And yet the fingers of that darkness were somehow leaking out of the cracks in his vault, willing to be aired out and seen even as the shame that accompanied that bleak memory arose as sharp and painful and throat-locking as it had been twenty years ago.

"Another time we'll talk about him," he lied with an apologetic caress against her jaw. "Tonight is yours. I refuse to spoil it with my messy family history."

A pulse of silence as she absorbed that, then her lashes came up again. The worst of the shadows were replaced with a teasing light.

"A fine aspiration when your mother has threatened to make an appearance."

In support, she had assured him, although Val knew it was also an attempt to catch a glimmer of Kiara's spotlight. Even so, the tightness in his chest eased as the tense moment between them passed.

"I will make that up to you, I swear."

The culmination of what felt like her life's work passed in a blur.

Val's celebrity and his mother's influence had magnified attention onto the event, turning it into a full-out media circus. Kiara walked a red carpet into the gallery, camera bulbs flashing like fireworks around her. Inside, she was introduced to rock stars and countesses and gallery curators from around the world.

Her agent and the gallery owner were beside themselves, glowing under their own brilliance in "discovering" her. The success of the night was a fait accompli.

Lest she be too humble, however, and attribute her success to Niko's patronage and

Val and Evelina's notoriety, and the gallery's name, and her agent's ruthless drive, an art critic known to be scathing caught her alone and gave her the best compliment of the night.

"I was convinced this was a stunt," he said in a bored, nasal tone. "Your husband is hardly above using his influence, and neither is his mother. But you're actually good. I'm buying the seascape tryptic. I don't buy art unless I believe it will appreciate. I certainly don't display it in my home unless I genuinely love it, and yours will take pride of place in my den, where I will see it every day."

"Thank you," she murmured, stunned and moved beyond words.

He was pulled away and she stood there a moment surrounded by the din of voices all talking about her, not to her. Feting her accomplishment without truly understanding what it meant to her.

In that second, all of this felt like a tremendously hollow victory. She had never felt more alone in her life and didn't understand why. She had done this. It had been her dream and here she was, living it. She ought to be euphoric.

Across the room, she caught Val's gaze on her. As they held the eye contact, he lifted his glass in a silent toast and she realized she wasn't alone. Her heart soared as she absorbed that he was here with her. Proud and genuinely happy for her.

She loved him for that.

Loved him.

Oh, dear. All of her realigned as the knowledge rippled through her. She loved him. Loved him, loved him, loved him.

That was good, wasn't it? He was her husband. The father of her child. He was enamored with their daughter and had become so very protective and generous toward her. They were making a life together.

But he didn't love her.

And all of a sudden, she was alone again.

She woke to rave reviews and the news from her agent that her show had sold out and there was a clamor for more.

Val congratulated her by pleasuring her

past mindless into a soaring climax that shattered her into a million pieces.

"Your sensuality is a glorious thing to behold, *bella*," he said huskily as he covered her and thrust into the flesh still singing with joy. "Is it because you're an artist? Or are you an artist because you live life with your whole body?"

"I can't talk when we're like this," she moaned, lost, utterly lost to the slow power of his body moving upon hers. Within her. Her own body responded to ancient signals and matched his rhythm, hips lifting to greet his. The buildup was steady and incredible, doubling and redoubling until she didn't know how she could withstand the tension, but she still wanted more and more and more.

This, she thought as they achieved utter synchronicity. It might not be love, but it was art.

In a swooping move, he hooked one strong arm behind her knee, and everything changed. The angle, the depth, the way his impact struck her nerve endings.

She cried out at the acute slam of pleasure that went through her and opened her eyes to the blinding gleam in his. The show of his clenched teeth.

His knowledge that she was *there* with him. His shoulders tensed and he thrust harder, coming with her as she fell off the cliff and discovered she could fly.

Over the next few weeks Val began to realize the hidden truth in that senseless expression "wedded bliss." He rather expected it was ignorance of the future, but he had to admit such blind contentment was enjoyable while it lasted.

When they were home, he and Kiara had fallen into a comfortable routine whereby he worked from the villa as often as he drove into Milan, and she disappeared into the guest cottage for a few hours every day to paint. When they traveled, they booked an extra day or two purely for family fun, spoiling Aurelia silly with days at the beach or amusement parks or other local attractions.

He was turning into that most tedious of animals, the domesticated married man. And despite eschewing all things conventional for most of his life, he was ridiculously smug in his role of husband and father.

"Slow down," he teased Kiara when they were eating breakfast the morning after a week in New York. "It will still be there in ten minutes."

Her baleful look made him chuckle.

"I think it's safe to assume your mother will not be joining us for lunch," he said to Aurelia.

"Why?" Aurelia stuffed a bite of crepe over her new favorite word.

"Because her studio is ready and she's excited to work in it. Shall we walk down with her to see it?"

Aurelia nodded and a few minutes later, they ambled through the dewy grass, Val particularly enjoying the way Kiara gasped and halted in her tracks when she saw his surprise.

"You are shameless," she declared of the small replica of her studio that had been placed a suitable distance from her own, far enough that a child's playful cries wouldn't be too distracting, but close enough she could see her daughter from her studio window.

Crouching, she pointed it out to Aurelia. "What is that? Who do you think that is for?"

"Me?" Aurelia took off in her wobbly gallop before she heard the answer.

"I always wanted a playhouse as a girl," Kiara said, looping her arm around his waist as they followed her. "Thank you for being such an indulgent father."

"Thank you for giving me someone to indulge." He kissed the tip of her nose, not sure if he meant his daughter or his wife.

So housebroken and not the least bit regretful, he acknowledged with bemusement.

Of course, his daughter was determined to humble him. She popped out of the little house with a crestfallen expression.

"Where's *my* paint?"

"Wow." Val nodded as he absorbed his own failing. "How did I not see that coming?"

"At least you're leaving room for *me* to be the hero sometimes," Kiara said with a teasing pinch of his side. "I'll order you some, lovey. Special paint for children. What else do you need?"

Kiara started to poke her head in and Aurelia stopped her with grave importance, holding up her palm. "You have to ask."

"Oh. Of course. May I come in?"

"Yes."

"Wonder where she got that from?" Val asked under his breath.

Kiara shot him a doleful look, but they cracked up as she disappeared into the house.

It was the most genuinely carefree moment he'd ever experienced. He wasn't forcing himself not to care, he merely felt all the heavier, darker cares fall away. They weren't important when he had this.

He would give these two females the blood and bones and breath from his body, he realized. There was nothing he could ever deny them.

Which was why he experienced such a schism of sheer agony when Kiara told him she wanted to leave him.

Kiara knew it was a big ask. More than that, it was a plea for trust. It was a test of this nascent, fragile, beautiful bond that was beginning to form between them.

"Javiero won't be there, just Scarlett and Locke. I'm not sure what's going on between them, but I'm worried about her. Being a new mother is hard and she was there for me—"

She cut herself off as he glanced at her, the dark admonishment still there that she hadn't leaned on *him* when she'd had Aurelia.

They had come a long way and most of her time with Niko was water under the bridge, but Val wouldn't listen to her complain about any struggles she'd had then when she hadn't even tried to reach out to him.

She swallowed. Tried a different tack. "I want to finish packing up my old studio." Hopefully, he would hear that as the permanent shift from her time with Niko to her life here with him that it was.

"You're not taking Aurelia."

She clenched her hands together. "Scarlett is the only auntie she has, Val. I know that doesn't sit well, but I didn't know Scarlett had an intimate relationship with Javiero until she told me she was pregnant, and he was the father."

"And if she keeps that sort of secret from

her supposed best friend…" He didn't finish, just left it hanging as a denunciation of Scarlett's character.

"You and I are not the only two people in this world who have painful things in our past," she said in a slightly sharper tone. "I haven't forced you to tell me about yours. Don't judge Scarlett for keeping her own pain to herself."

"What does that mean?" Val's head snapped around. "What did Javiero do to her?"

"Nothing. I mean…" She sighed. "Look, she didn't tell me much about their relationship and I don't like betraying what she did confide, but I guess she saw him occasionally, the same way she turned up to badger you on Niko's behalf. You didn't ever sleep with her, did you?" she blurted with low horror as it occurred to her.

He glared. "That's beneath you."

It was an ironic remark from a man who had prided himself on acting inappropriately, but his mouth twisted as he admitted, "I flirted in the early days, more to test her loyalty than anything. The fact she stuck by

Dad so unwaveringly made her less and less attractive to me as time wore on."

"Yes, well, I gather that was the bone of contention between her and your brother. Javiero expected her to leave Niko for him and she refused."

The curl of disgust at the corner of his lips deepened. "Poor Javiero."

"I'm worried about how things have been going between them, Val."

They don't have what you and I do, she wanted to add, but she wasn't sure what they had. She was terrified of making a false move that would somehow damage his regard. "Javiero isn't there. She said they needed a break and I get the feeling he's like you and hates the island."

"Never again assume that he and I are alike in any way," he warned dangerously.

"Fine, but you and he still have a relationship that goes beyond hating one another!" She shot to her feet in agitation. "Javiero is Aurelia's blood relative. Do you realize that? And *you* have a nephew. Locke is your daughter's cousin and I will risk your wrath to give our children a better relationship than you have with your *equally pigheaded* half brother."

"Pigheaded? The man lacks a basic moral compass," he snarled. "He had a chance to do the right thing and he *didn't*."

She halted and let her own ruffled feathers settle to make room for the barbed bristles shooting off him.

"Val, what happened?" she asked with pent-up anguish.

His face filled with the bleak rage she'd seen the day of the will reading, when they had dined on the rooftop in Athens before going to the hospital.

"It doesn't matter," he muttered, surging to his feet. "Go then. Before I change my mind. Be back within the week or I'm coming to get you. And he had better not come anywhere near either of you."

Scarlett burst into tears when Kiara arrived and so did Kiara. When Kiara held sweet-smelling Locke, her ovaries throbbed with longing. Maybe, she thought yearningly, but

Val wasn't ready to talk about more children. He was barely talking to her at all.

She and Scarlett didn't have that problem. At first, they couldn't talk fast enough. Scarlett wanted a blow-by-blow on how the gallery showing had gone and where Kiara's career was taking her. She spared no details about her labor and Locke's colicky start and how little sleep she was getting.

But slowly, slowly, as the children were put to bed and they shared a bottle of Niko's best vintage, Scarlett began to cry.

And cry.

She cried so hard Kiara feared she wouldn't stop.

"I think she's suffering postpartum," Kiara told Val over a hushed video chat from her studio a few days later. "I'm trying to convince her to see a doctor and helping with Locke as much as she'll let me, but she's so stubborn, convinced she has to do everything herself. She's pushing herself way too hard."

"How much longer are you staying?"

"I'm not sure," she said apologetically, moving quickly as she spoke, boxing up items without her usual care. "I'm only coming in here when everyone is napping, trying to spend as much time with Scarlett as possible. It sounds like things have been a struggle with Javiero's family. A few more days at least."

He didn't bother hiding his scowl of dismay.

A knock at the door had her glancing up to see a maid waving toward the landline extension on the wall.

"*Señor* Rodriguez is asking for you," the maid said.

"You said he wasn't there!" Val snapped.

"He isn't! He's on the phone," she hurried to clarify, but had to text him a few minutes later or risk his thinking she was hiding things from him.

Javiero is coming by boat in the morning. He won't stay on the island but insists on seeing Scarlett.

She paused, loath to say it, but she had to.

I can't leave her to face him alone.

Val didn't respond.

* * *

"That's him," Scarlett said in an ominous, hollow tone the next morning while they ate their breakfast on the terrace.

A yacht had appeared on the horizon and it was headed straight toward them. Kiara had the sense of panic ancient people must have felt when the enemy ship appeared and there was nowhere to run. They could only wait, hearts in their throats, for feet to reach land.

When Kiara had spoken to Javiero yesterday, she had discovered he and Val had both inherited Niko's streak of unstoppable single-mindedness. He was coming whether Scarlett was ready to see him or not, bringing his own accommodation so he could wait her out if necessary.

"If you don't want to see him, you don't have to," Kiara reminded her, even though she had no serious means of stopping him if he wanted to push past her.

Scarlett seemed to realize that. She made a noise of hysterical amusement and brought Locke to her shoulder, yanking her robe closed as she did.

"I'll burp him. You can shower and put your best face on." Or go back to bed, Kiara wanted to urge, frowning with concern at Scarlett's bruised eyes and translucent skin.

Scarlett hadn't slept last night, worried about this coming confrontation. She wasn't likely to rest now, however, since Javiero was almost here.

"I can do it," Scarlett insisted absently.

"I want to hold him while I have the chance," Kiara said truthfully, but she also knew a gentle guilt trip was about the only way she could persuade Scarlett to give herself a break.

Scarlett was refusing to let the nannies do more than restock the diapers and fold laundry, terrified she wasn't bonding with her son properly. Kiara had a feeling it was Scarlett who was struggling with her feelings, not the contented baby who settled every time he was in his mother's arms.

Scarlett was in a bad way, convinced she was merely tired and upset about an argument she'd had with Paloma. Kiara suspected there was more to it and doubted Javiero would be anything but added stress. She intended to take Scarlett to see her old doctor while they were here.

"I'll put him down if he falls asleep," Kiara promised, holding out her hands.

"Thank you," Scarlett murmured with defeat, handing across the infant and drifting into the house after a last conflicted look at the approaching boat.

Kiara had just finished settling the dozing infant and agreed with the nanny that yes, Aurelia could watch her show for a few minutes, when she heard the unmistakable *rat-a-tat* of an approaching helicopter.

The world stopped. She knew instinctively who it was. Her pulse began to throb in time to the rotors. Both excitement and anticipation of disaster whirled within her.

She hurried to the terrace. The yacht had come as close as it dared. A smaller boat had been launched and was headed to the private pier.

She turned and shaded her eyes. The helicopter was closing in.

It was a slow-motion collision that she couldn't watch. She ran inside to warn Scarlett.

Seconds later Kiara was changing from her yoga pants and T-shirt into a decent dress when the muffled sound of the landing helicopter rumbled the stone walls of the villa. She hurried to the stairs and exchanged an apprehensive look with Scarlett as they trotted down and out to the terrace.

As they emerged, a sound like snarling wolves filled the air.

"Oh, my God," Kiara murmured as she saw the men.

They had met on the lawn between the stairs to the beach and the path around the house. They were both puffed up, locked in a clash of wills, ready to come to blows.

"Val," Kiara shouted and hurried down the steps toward them.

"Get Aurelia. We're leaving," Val bit out, holding his half brother's gaze in the way she'd seen him do at the hospital. They were practically nose to nose, teeth bared by their curled lips. "If Scarlett can't survive without you, she can come with us."

"Don't even think—" Javiero started to lunge.

Kiara threw herself between them.

"Stop!" she cried, arms out to hold them apart even as Val gripped her by the shoulders and tried to move her aside. "For the sake of your babies, stop acting like children. Bury the hatchet," she insisted.

"Let me just turn around so you can get it in beside your *knife*," Javiero sneered, thumbing over his shoulder.

"Me? I stabbed *you* in the back?" Val asked with outraged astonishment.

"You know you did."

"When?"

"Don't play dumb, Val. She's right about one thing." Javiero stabbed a finger toward Kiara. "We're far too old for this." Javiero looked old. Tired. Haggard and defeated as he let his attention flicker to the terrace where Scarlett stood frozen and pale.

"I'm serious," Val muttered. "What the hell

did I ever do to you to deserve what you did to me?"

"I've never done a damned thing to you," Javiero roared, turning back on him with aggression that sought a target that wasn't a fragile woman who'd given birth two short months ago.

"You've never done anything *for* me, either. Have you?" Val charged, the disillusionment in his face stopping Kiara's heart.

Her hand instinctively tried to soothe by moving against his chest, but he brushed her hand away.

Javiero faltered. His mouth tightened. "You're blaming me for the bullies at school? I was a child, Val. I didn't ask for anyone to behave that way and I told them to stop. They weren't my friends. I didn't pile in. The administration should have taken steps. You didn't need to cut my entire family loose over it."

"I cut *myself* loose," Val said with a knock of his fist into the middle of his own chest. "I told you to take all of this." He flung out his hand to encompass the island. "Don't put it on me that you refused it."

"Nice fairy tale you've told yourself. Dad wasn't about to leave his fortune to the weaker son who *wasn't* capable of supporting himself. How the hell was I supposed to do that at *thirteen*?" Javiero scoffed. "My family sat on the brink of ruin for a *decade* because of your precious need to stick it to everyone around you. So screw you very much for that. Now, get the hell out of my way because I want to see my son."

"Don't you pin that on me. If you had backed me up when you had the chance, I might have made other choices, but you didn't. I had every right to walk away. I *had* to," Val bit out in a graveled, bitter tone. "You know I did."

"How the hell was I supposed to—" Javiero's enraged face blanked.

The air changed and Val's emanation of fury seemed to flip on itself, turning into a shield of wariness. All his defenses had come down like a wall, one that slammed his expression blank. One that pushed both of them to some perimeter where they couldn't touch him.

She looked to Javiero for a clue. He had gone ghostly gray beneath his naturally swarthy skin. The fading pink scratches on his face stood out as bright and angry as they'd been the day Kiara had seen him at the hospital.

"That was real?" Javiero asked in a rasp.

If Kiara hadn't been tunneling her way around the door to his vault all these weeks, it wouldn't have snapped open the way it had. Suddenly, there was Javiero, his worst enemy, staring in shock at Val's deepest shame.

Somehow, when Val had believed that Javiero knew the truth all along, and had preferred to beat him with it, he had been able to bear it far more easily than seeing horror and something like compunction dawn on his half brother's face.

The naked boy in him shrank but had nowhere to hide. And when Kiara touched him and said, "Val?" she might as well have branded him. Amputated his arm. Torn him asunder.

Anger at being disbelieved had always been his sword. Without that bitter resentment to deflect the world, he had to snatch up other excuses to lash out, otherwise shame would settle on him and smother him to death.

"You said he wouldn't be here," he said, rounding on Kiara. "If you're not in the helicopter by the time I get there, you're not coming."

"Val!" She trotted after him as he strode away. "Talk to me. Tell me what's going on."

"I don't have to tell you anything. Do you understand that?"

She backed up a step, her fear of him so tangible he tasted its coppery flavor on his tongue.

He hated himself then. Hated the poison in him that festered to this day. Hated what he was and that he hadn't been able to stop turning into this.

"You've made your choice, Kiara," he said with a chuck of his chin toward the villa and Javiero and Niko's haunting presence.

"That's not true," she said, hand coming up, but she stopped short of trying to touch him again. "I choose you, Val. Always. I love you."

He couldn't bear to look at her then. She couldn't love him. *Couldn't.* Not if she knew.

"Love is a lie, Kiara. It's something people say to get what they want. My lawyers will be in touch about visitation."

He walked away.

CHAPTER EIGHT

KIARA WAS GUTTED. *Lawyers?*

Her love wasn't a lie. It was as vast as the horizon. As wide as the sky Val rose into the air seconds later, while she stood there paralyzed by agony, emotions filleted by the punishing blades of the helicopter.

Her love wasn't something he wanted, though. *She* wasn't, either.

A scuff behind her had her flinging around. Javiero was starting toward the terrace and Scarlett was disappearing into the house.

"Javiero," Kiara said through a raw throat. "You have to tell me."

He paused and cast her a glance of angry distraction. She saw the struggle in him as he wanted to follow Scarlett, but at the last second he relented. He ran his hand down his face.

"I don't even know what to make of it." He looked to where the helicopter had become a speck in the sky.

"Of what? I love him. He's hurting. He's been hurting for *decades*. What *happened*?"

He flinched and the weight of guilt seemed to slump his shoulders.

"There was a teacher. A woman. Yes," he said as her eyes widened. "You have to remember how Val looked at thirteen. The image he projected. That's not blame," he hurried to add, lifting a hand to keep her from interrupting. "I'm just trying to explain how a woman three times his age might have seen a young man, not a boy. Not that it excuses her behavior."

Kiara covered her mouth and shook her head, certain she didn't want to hear the rest, but for Val's sake she had to.

"I don't know much, only rumors. I thought—" Remorse dug deeper lines into his disfigured face. "As a man, I can see how wrong it was. If the roles had been reversed, there would be no question that a man chasing a young girl was utterly disgusting.

Deeply unequal. At the time, given our age, our history… I'm ashamed to say I thought that his getting with a teacher sounded like something he would do. He was always very confident, Kiara. I didn't become this obdurate by being pitted against a pushover. Until a minute ago, it didn't fit in my head that something like that would be anything but his choice."

"Well, you were wrong," she said with subdued outrage, heart aching for Val. "Is that what you told Niko? Is that why Val thinks you didn't back him up when he needed you to?"

Javiero made a helpless gesture with his hand.

"Dad asked me whether anything was going on between them. I told him the truth, that I hadn't seen anything, only heard other boys tease him because she flirted openly with him in class."

"What did Niko do? Anything?" she asked desperately.

Javiero drew a deep, pained breath. "He

said, 'Well, I guess your brother is a man now. When will *you* become one?'"

She rocked on her feet. Why did that surprise her after all she'd heard about the old man?

"That's disgusting," she choked. "You're saying he believed it happened, he just didn't believe it was wrong? Did he try to put a stop to it?"

"She continued to teach after Val had been expelled so I don't imagine he said a word to anyone about it."

I had every right to walk away.

"I have to go home," she said, mind skipping over the things she still needed to pack, but all she really needed was to collect their daughter and hurry to Val's side.

No wonder he had struggled to forgive her for relying on his father. She could barely stand herself right now.

Her heart skidded into the dirt as she recalled why she was here, though.

"Javiero, we need to talk about Scarlett."

He paused with one foot on the steps to the terrace and cast her another impatient look.

"She doesn't want to get married, I know," he said through his teeth. "But they're coming home with me."

"It's not about that. She needs a doctor."

Val had no one left to hate. No one left to punish.

Even his mother failed him in his time of need. She called while he was pretending to work in London, where he had told his PA not to disturb him so he could glower broodingly at the pouring rain beyond his skyscraper window.

Evelina, being Evelina, talked the young woman into risking her job and putting the call through.

He wouldn't have picked up, he realized as he heard her voice, but he had expected a different one. Had *wanted* to hear a different one. He longed for Kiara's lilting intonation, even if she was calling to tell him their marriage was over.

"Your wife is wondering where you are," Evelina stated.

"Then give her this number."

"She seems a soft touch where you're concerned. I'm better versed in handling you when you're in one of your moods."

"Mmm, no one could accuse you of possessing an ounce of tenderness, could they?"

"Take your shots, Val. You always will, but are you really going to throw away a marriage that has every chance of long-term success?"

He snorted. "Hang on to Dad's money is what you're saying. And don't kick her out because she'll kick you out."

"I'm saying she's a surprisingly laudable addition to our family. Who knew she possessed such talent?"

"I did. I knew," he couldn't help asserting.

"And she's not forever seeking the front page with a fresh part in her hair the way what's-her-name was given to doing." Read: Kiara posed little threat to Evelina's ability to garner attention.

"What do you want, Mother?" he asked wearily.

"I want you to go home to your wife, of course."

He wanted that, too. It was an ache he couldn't seem to quash, but he didn't know how to face her.

"She's not home. She's on the island."

"She's at your villa," she informed as if he ought to know that. "Has been for days, awaiting your return like a stalwart shepherd."

"Do *not* refer to her like that again or I will cut you off completely."

"I only meant she is blind to your faults and far more patient with your petty behavior than you deserve."

His chest was tightening as he thought of her in their bed. Something that might have been homesickness washed over him.

"Val, it's time we put the past behind us," Evelina said firmly.

"Ha!" he barked out. "You really just said that? To *me*?"

"You know damned well why I had to fight so hard for everything I have," she said sharply. "What I cannot understand is why you fight so hard to throw *away* all that you have."

You know why, he wanted to shout. But they'd had that conversation once and he hadn't liked her response. It had made him feel all the more powerless and sickened by life.

"Goodbye, Mother."

"Go to her," she insisted.

He hung up, the words *I'll do what I want* unspoken.

Because what he wanted was to follow his mother's directive. He swore at the ceiling, hating that his good, reliable, self-destructive tendencies were no longer as easy to fall back on. There had been a time when going in the opposite direction of wherever he was being sent had been the most satisfying of actions.

It was no longer that simple. No, if he really wanted to burn down his marriage, then he would have to go back to Kiara and do it properly. Show her his soul and let her kick it to the curb once and for all.

Kiara finally understood why she'd never been able to paint Val. She hadn't known exactly how she felt about him.

She did now. She loved him. So much it engulfed her like a spell, compelling her to make him appear on her canvas. She took days to get her sketches right, working from the Venice ones and a handful of photos on her phone and her myriad store of memories, built over the two months they'd been married.

When she came to render him in oils, she considered the affectionate expression he wore when he gazed at their daughter and the killer seductive gaze he often leveled at her. That one that curled her toes every time and she adored it. She even played with the cynical curve of his mouth when his mood was light and the glower he wore when the world and the people around him failed him in some way.

Ultimately, she settled on a very familiar, austere three-quarter profile. This was the man she knew best. The one who kept his thoughts and feelings well hidden behind his mask of undeniable, classic male beauty.

She knew what that mask hid, though, and those deep hurts made her take great care with her brush strokes, as if she could somehow heal his aches and disappointments and betrayals with each caress of sable to his smooth skin.

"Papà!"

Kiara's heart leaped out of her chest and she almost bobbled her brush into her canvas. She hurried to the door of her studio in time to see Val bend and scoop their daughter off her feet as she ran toward him.

The nanny hovered awkwardly, but Kiara held up a hand to signal she should stay. She wanted her to take their daughter so she and Val could talk. She would give them time for their reunion first, though.

"I mitt you!" Aurelia told him in a scold, pulling her arms from around his neck and taking his unshaven cheeks into her tiny starfished hands.

"I missed you, too," he said, voice not quite steady as his gaze ate up her little face.

She tilted her head and lifted an imploring shoulder to ask sweetly, "Can we swim? *Per favore*?" She used Italian, the minx, because she had learned that nearly always got her what she wanted out of him.

"Later," he promised with a rueful smile and pecked a kiss onto her button nose. "After your lunch and nap *if* you do both without a fuss." He tucked his chin so his gaze was level with hers. "Deal?"

Aurelia copied his very serious chin tuck, stating firmly, "Deal."

"*Grazie.* Now please go with Nanny. I need to speak with Mummy."

She gave his neck another squeeze, then let him set her on her feet and skipped up to the villa.

When Kiara dragged her eyes off their daughter, she clashed into Val's unreadable gaze. It knocked the breath out of her to see shades of that same greedy hunger he'd exhibited with Aurelia, as though he had been starving for the sight of her as well as his daughter.

"She's been asking for you," she said, not knowing what else to say.

"I got those texts. I thought we agreed we

wouldn't use her as emotional blackmail against each other."

She bit her lip, guilty as charged, but, "It was true."

She realized she was still holding her brush and moved into her studio to drop it into the jar of solvent next to her easel. Her hand was shaking.

He followed her in, uninvited, as was his habit. And, much as she hated for anyone to see her work in process, she had come to trust that his circumspect study of her unfinished work would never be critical or hurtful.

Today was different, though. This portrait was different. *They* were different.

He swore as he saw his own image. Swore and ran his hand down his face and sounded both defeated and…moved? "You've been busy."

He backed up to the sofa he'd had brought in there "so we have a comfortable place to make love." She'd told him he was dreaming, then had blinds installed in her wall of windows.

"What am I supposed to think of that?" he

asked in a graveled voice as he continued to stare at his portrait. He braced his elbows on his thighs, fingers clawed into his hair.

She looked at it, thinking it was some of her best work, even though it laid her heart so bare. She had essentially rolled it out onto the floor for him to walk across.

"I missed you and wanted to see you. I—"

"You love me. Yes, I can see that, Kiara."

His harsh words went straight into her chest like an arrow.

"The things you feel are always right there, on every single canvas." He pointed his flat hand at his image in a type of accusation. "I see it and hear it and feel it, but there's no way you can love me. Not that much. Not—" He cut himself off, seeming utterly vanquished as he threw his head into his hands again, tortured by whatever was gripping him.

"I do, Val," she swore gently as she moved to sit beside him. "I love you so much it feels like a bruise inside me, throbbing all the time. And it's okay if you don't feel the same."

Her artist's eye studied him as he looked again at himself and she smiled a little at how perfectly she'd captured that particular mask he wore as he tried to suppress all that was going on inside him.

"I mean, I hope you feel something," she whispered. "But—"

"Kiara," he chided, looking at her now with such agony in his gaze her swollen heart felt pinched in a vise.

She wanted to take his hands, but wasn't sure if he would welcome it, not when they had to go into painful places inside him. Places he had spent a lifetime navigating alone.

She swallowed and spoke tentatively. "I can imagine why love feels like a lie to you when people who were supposed to love you let you down. More than once. I didn't mean to."

"Javiero told you." He closed his eyes, shutting her out.

"Only what he knew, which wasn't much." She didn't want to defend Javiero, but nor did she want to stoke Val's animosity toward him. "He did tell Niko there were rumors, but that was all he knew, Val. I'm so sorry that happened to you. That Niko didn't do anything to stop it. It was wrong and it wasn't your fault."

"Wasn't it? I didn't exactly fight her off." He pushed the heels of his hands into his eye sockets. His sigh was jagged and heavy. Tormented. "I was selling sex to the cameras. I knew I was. Everything around me told me I was supposed to want what she was offering. So I went along with it and felt *sick*."

"You were too young and inexperienced to know how you were supposed to act or feel. That's not your fault. She was the adult, Val. It was her responsibility to see that acting that way was wrong and not do it. *Niko* should have seen that. He should have had her fired. Arrested."

Val made a choking noise and dropped his hands to let them dangle loosely between his knees. "Dad thought I was a damned hero for losing my virginity so young. He was proud."

He wasn't looking at her. His cheeks were stained with disgrace.

"Niko was wrong," she said as firmly as her unsteady voice could manage. "I don't blame you for hating him, Val. Parents are supposed to keep their children safe, not send them to predators." She frowned, prying very gently. "Did your mother know?"

Despair filled his gaze and the noise he made was utterly defeated. "She said, 'How do you think I got where I am? That's how the game is played.'"

"Oh, my God."

"Exactly." He turned his head to look at her with concern. "Have you ever...?"

"I've had my share of difficult experiences. Nothing violent, just the wrong sort of attention. Catcalls." Landlords and employers who said inappropriate things. Teachers who commented on her developing body. *The usual*, she wanted to call it, but sighed instead.

"That's why I support her," Val said broodingly. "Financially. That's why she's still part of my life even though she makes me crazy. I'm fairly certain what I went through was nothing compared to what she faced at different times in her life. There was a stepfather she refuses to talk about, and she moved to Paris alone at fifteen. If she's self-serving and incapable of genuine connection or anything that resembles empathy, I'm sure she has her reasons."

"That's sad," Kiara murmured.

"She pointed out something to me, though." He rubbed his thighs. "While she was busy trying to save my marriage so you wouldn't yank the money you're giving her. That was a dirty move, by the way. Siccing her on me like that. It's the sort of merciless attack I would use to get what I want."

"I was genuinely worried about you." *And* inclined to believe that Evelina would be strongly motivated to interfere in the best possible way. "What did she say?"

"She drew my attention to the fact she had fought long and hard to climb out of being victimized. She has never said it in so many words, but I've had time to realize how badly Dad took advantage of her, exactly like damned near every man she'd ever encountered. She was in her late twenties, worried her career would begin to fade, when Dad said he was breaking things off to marry Paloma. She did the only thing she thought she could to finally have some power and agency. I don't agree with it, but I see why she did it. Then here I was, born into power and money. Influence. And because I felt victimized, I spent years trying to break away from it. That doesn't make sense."

"You were angry. Understandably."

"But I had convinced myself I didn't feel anything. And that's the thing about emotions. You can't pick and choose what to feel. It's all or nothing. You have to take the bad with the good and when the bad is really bad?"

She nodded, heart sinking. "I understand. You need to protect yourself."

"I want to. But when something feels really good, it's hard to resist letting it happen." He sighed and looked to the ceiling but opened his palm to her. "The way I feel about you... There aren't enough words, Kiara. I wish I could paint. I wish you could see what I see when I look at you. When I touch you."

Oh. She set her hand in his and his warm grip closed over her fingers, injecting a sensation of pure joy up her arm and into her heart.

"It's not fair for me to say that love is a lie. I said that because I had never experienced it so I thought it didn't exist. Then Aurelia—"

His eyes were damp as he met hers, and her own suffered a fresh sting of tears. They exchanged a knowing smile, both so powerfully smitten with their girl that only the other could possibly understand the intensity of love she inspired.

"She's pretty amazing, isn't she?" Kiara choked.

"She is pure magic. And I have to give you credit for that because her brand of pureness did not come from me."

"Please don't talk about yourself like that."

"I've still been a bastard in many ways," he said, bringing her hand to his lips.

"And I still love you. Exactly as you are. So much."

"And I love you, Kiara. I love that you take your own pain and turn it into something beautiful. I love that fighting back is your last resort, not your first, but you'll do it when you have to. I love that you rock my world when we're in bed."

"You rock mine," she countered wryly.

"That's what does it for me," he said throatily, but sobered as he added gravely, "I love that you make our lovemaking feel right. That's precious to me. *You* are precious to me."

Oh. She sniffled, only becoming aware that her eyes were leaking when the tickling sensation brought her hand up to brush her emotive tears from her cheeks. She could hardly bear the pressure in her chest and throat, but she exulted in it at the same time.

"I don't believe in fate, but I do believe you are the only woman who could have brought me out of the darkness like this. I want to be the better man who deserves you. I love you with everything in me and I'm going to stop fighting it. I'm going to embrace what we have."

"I just want you to embrace me—oh!"

He grabbed her onto his lap and tumbled her down into the sofa cushions at the same time, kissing her surprised mouth with his smile.

"I am going to embrace the hell out of you.

We have an entire week's worth of lovemaking to make up for." He lifted enough to open the buttons on her smock, glancing at the back of his fingers as he picked up a smear of the cerulean blue she'd mixed with titanium white to match his eyes.

"Remember to save some strength for your swim this afternoon," she teased, filtering her fingers through his thick hair.

His eyes, which she'd gotten exactly right with her shade of icy blue, came up to stare with disgruntlement into hers. "Whose dumb idea was it to promise *that*?"

"I don't know. A man who is far more generous and thoughtful than he would want anyone to believe, I think."

"I do have a brand to protect." He rearranged them so he was between her denim-clad thighs.

"Your chewy caramel center will be our little secret," she whispered, tracing the lips that were making her strain with longing beneath him. "But speaking of keeping secrets…" She arched her neck as his mouth dipped to nibble against her throat.

He brought his head up abruptly, face blanked with shock. "Are you pregnant?"

"What? *No*. I was just going to ask you to close the blinds so people don't see what we're doing in here."

"Oh." The way his expression fell had her clasping his shoulders to keep him atop her as he started to push up.

"Wait. Did you *want* me to be pregnant?" she asked with a dip and roll of her heart.

His tongue ran over his teeth behind his closed lips as he considered.

"I think I did." He nodded slowly. "I'm pretty sure I'm disappointed. But let's save that conversation for when we have more time." He dropped a kiss onto her mouth then rose to drop the blinds. "Right now I only have two short hours before I'm due with a toddler in a swimming pool and I want to make the most of it."

And they did.

EPILOGUE

Two years later...

KIARA BLINKED SLEEPY eyes at him and sounded as petulant as their daughter did when she was resisting bedtime.

"I don't want to sleep. I want to look at him."

"I'll look at him for both of us," Val said, cupping her cheek tenderly and dropping a soft kiss on her pouted mouth before he stole their swaddled and sleeping son from her arms. "You need to rest. That was a lot of work you did."

Watching Kiara deliver Rafael had been the most singularly overwhelming experience of his life, and Val had only witnessed his wife pushing their son into this world. She was the one who had labored long and hard to make it happen. He was so proud of her. So proud of their son. So happy he couldn't describe it, only revel in it.

"You're tired, too," she said on a yawn. "Lie with me." She scooted over a little in the narrow hospital bed.

He *was* tired. Apparently, babies didn't always arrive at a civilized dinner hour the way Locke had. Sometimes they woke you at midnight and made their appearance at dawn.

"I'll hold you until you fall asleep," he promised, settling their son in his bassinet in case he dozed off himself. He had every intention of rising, though. That tiny boy was a magnet pulling his cast-iron heart out of his body.

"I should text Scarlett," Kiara murmured as Val settled beside her. She snuggled her head onto his shoulder.

"I'll do it," Val promised, thinking he understood now why Javiero had been such a jackass that day. The only other person Val could stomach entering their tiny bubble of contentment was the daughter who was probably not even awake yet, but who had impatiently been waiting for her little brother or sister to arrive.

"Val?"

"Yes, my love?" He caressed her upper arm.

"I'm really glad you were here this time."

"Me, too." He turned his head to kiss her brow. "You were incredible."

"You, too."

He snorted and picked up her hand to kiss her fingertips. "You give me too much credit, *bella*, but I shall continue to do my best."

She made a little noise of contentment, arm growing heavy on his waist as she drifted into sleep.

Meanwhile, he drew the bassinet a little closer to the bed so he could see the small miracle they had made together.

* * * * *

LET'S TALK

Romance

For exclusive extracts, competitions
and special offers, find us online:

f facebook.com/millsandboon

⌾ @millsandboonuk

🐦 @millsandboon

Or get in touch on 0844 844 1351*

For all the latest titles coming soon,
visit millsandboon.co.uk/nextmonth

*Calls cost 7p per minute plus your phone company's price per
minute access charge